MW00945439

Something
I'm
Good
At

A
Sol del Mar High
Novel

Caroline Andrus

For my sister Katie Schumacher,
my friend Alisha Webster, and anyone else living
with a lifelong illness.

Stay strong.

"I have this theory of convergence that good things always happen with bad things."

- SAY ANYTHING, 1989

1

KANE

In the sixteen years I've been on this earth, I've discovered there are a lot of things I'm no good at: Boy Scouts, football, soccer—team sports in general—not getting food all over myself when I eat. The list goes on. But today is going to be different.

I'm wearing my lucky t-shirt, the blue one with the cartoon taco that says, "I'm Into Fitness. Fit'ness Taco In My Mouth." I need all the luck I can get, because *today* I'm saying goodbye to the low practice flatrails at the Sol del Mar Skatepark. Against my friend's advice, I'm attempting to grind the real handrails.

My best friends, Mark and Abigail, are nearby watching. They've been grinding the rails for ages, while I've been left behind. Well, no more. Ignoring the blazing August sun roasting me alive, I adjust my sunglasses and focus on the rail in front of me. I visualize myself nailing the grind. I'll ollie up at a 45 degree angle, keep my balance, and slide my board down the length of the rail. This will be a cakewalk.

"There's no way you're going to get this. You're not ready," Mark calls out. His face—what I can see of it behind his dark sunglasses—is serious, and I know he's only looking out for my safety. Mark and I have been tight since we were practically in diapers. We used to be next door neighbors. We even got matching haircuts recently—shaved close on the sides and longer on top. Somehow it looks way cooler on him than me.

"Aw...leave him alone, Mark," Abigail says. Though I don't take their ribbing to heart, it is refreshing to hear one of them have faith in me for once. "I like watching Kane fall."

So much for that.

Tuning them out, I take one more deep breath and put my board in motion. I aim for a small ramp and lean into a turn, gaining speed as I shoot down the incline. The rail is just up ahead. I count the seconds in my head, then kick my board up into the ollie. I land on the rail and grin as I hear the sweet sound of metal on metal.

"Nailed it!" I yell, pumping my fist in the air.

And then I lose it. Next thing I know, I'm falling face first, the hot concrete rushing toward me. I quickly bring both arms up to break my fall and protect my face, and I land hard on my right wrist. Pain shoots through my hand and up the length of the arm.

Rolling onto my back, I clutch my arm and yell, "Son of a bitch!" It's either that or cry, and no way am I crying in front of my friends and everyone else at the skatepark.

Footsteps pound the pavement, and I know my friends are running toward me. Right arm clutched to my chest, I squeeze my eyes tight against the pain and the blinding sun. So much for my lucky t-shirt. I'm 98.3 percent sure I've broken my wrist.

The bright sun against my closed eyelids is suddenly eclipsed, and when I open them, my friends are hovering above me. They wear matching expressions: unimpressed and unsurprised.

Mark pushes his sunglasses up into his light brown hair and shakes his head. "I told you man, if you'd tried the 50-50 first you could have jumped out of that fall."

"Is his wrist supposed to bend that way?" Abigail asks. One

side of her lip is curled up in disgust as she nibbles the black polish from one of her thumb nails.

"Not. Helping," I bite back through clenched teeth. "Help me up. And then drive me to urgent care."

I know better than to go to the emergency room. After my third break, Mom got the bill and told me to quit being stupid and stop injuring myself. Then—because she knows me—she added that if I *was* going to be stupid, at least do her bank account a favor and get myself to urgent care instead.

Mark grasps my uninjured hand and helps me to my feet, while Abigail retrieves my skateboard. I keep my right arm close to my body and my head down as I walk through the skatepark. I ignore the commotion of the other skaters still riding the ramps and rails.

We step through the open arch of the entrance. It's a huge thing with SOL DEL MAR SKATEPARK spelled out across the top in twisted metal. It was probably really cool once, but now it's old and rusted.

"You've got a little something on your face." I glance to my right. Dennis, one of the regulars at the skatepark, is sitting on the crumbling brick wall next to the arch. He's pointing at his chin, a lit cigarette between his fingers. The big dopey grin on his face tells me he's probably high.

I pause and swipe at my chin. My hand comes away red with blood. "Thanks."

"No prob, K-man."

I wave goodbye to Dennis and continue walking. We reach Mark's gray Subaru. Three feet from the vehicle, Mark puts his hand up in the universal sign for stop. He rummages in the front seat for a moment, then emerges with a wad of tissues.

"If you get blood all over my seat, so help me Kane..." Mark lets the threat hang. I know he's kidding. Mostly. His parents gave him their used car for his sixteenth birthday. The only thing he loves more is his surfboard.

I grunt to let him know I heard and press the tissue into the wound on my chin. I'm careful not to smear blood anywhere when I climb into the backseat.

While Mark and Abigail climb in, I drop the tissue to my lap and pull my phone from my front pocket. I call Mom's cell, then wedge the phone between my shoulder and ear, grab the tissue, and press it to my chin again. Glancing around, I realize I've dripped blood on my shorts. At least I missed Mark's upholstery.

She picks up after three rings and says, "What happened?"

"Hello to you too, Mother," I quip back, trying to keep things lighthearted.

She sighs. "Kane..."

"I'm not going to the ER," I tell her, a hopeful cadence to my voice.

"Urgent care?" she says, her voice dry.

"...Yes."

Mom sighs again. "I'll meet you there."

"Thanks, Mom."

"Give me some warning; what is it? Leg? Arm? Head?"

"Wrist."

"I should throw that skateboard in the trash."

"You know I'd just get another."

Mom releases yet another sigh. I know I'm exasperating her, but I can't help it.

I hang up with my mom and shove the phone back in my pocket. Abigail turns up the radio so loud I can't even hear myself think. Before long, we're pulling into the parking lot of the Sol del Mar Urgent Care. Mark hits the speed bump in the lot too fast and my arm slams into the door. I curse and bite back the pain. I think I hear Mark mumble an apology, but it's hard to tell over the earsplitting music.

As the three of us climb out, I bump my arm yet again on the door frame. Wincing, I close my eyes against the pain, then slam the door closed behind me—harder than necessary—earning me a frown from Mark. I ignore him and glare at the car. Stupid door.

We enter the all too familiar building, and I step in line behind a woman with a little boy. I wait as the woman at the desk hands the mother a clipboard of paperwork. The mother leads the crying toddler to a set of chairs to our right. When the desk is clear, I step forward, and the woman looks up.

She raises her eyebrows, looks me over, and says, "I wondered when we'd be seeing you again, Mr. Dwyer."

I shrug, and the small movement sends pain shooting through my wrist. I flinch. "I just can't stay away, Patricia."

She sighs—that seems to be my superpower, making middle-aged women sigh. I think I'm up to four for the day. She clips a pen to a clipboard and hands it to me. "Looks like you ripped up your chin." She looks me up and down. "And your arm?"

"Pretty sure I broke my wrist." I cock my head to one side, not making the mistake of shrugging again. I'm sure I look super awkward, especially since I'm still holding the wad of blood soaked tissues to my chin.

Patricia shakes her head. "Go ahead and start filling this out if you can. Is your mom on her way?"

"Yep." I reach for the clipboard with the tissue hand and Patricia grimaces. Mark steps forward and grabs the clipboard before I can. Patricia shoos us away.

I retreat to the waiting area on the left—away from the crying kid—and take a seat. The blue plastic chairs are hard and uncomfortable, as if waiting to see a doctor wasn't painful enough. My friends settle in on either side of me.

"You guys can take off; this could take a while."

"Try not to fall off the exam table, okay?" Abigail stands and sets my skateboard on her vacated seat. I stick my tongue out at her.

Mark shakes his head and sets the clipboard down beside him. "When are you going to start listening to me, man?" Before I can whip out a witty comeback, he stands as well and laughs. "Text when they spring you from this joint."

"Will do."

My friends give one last wave goodbye before vacating the building. I glance around at the other inmates. There are only a handful, which means this will hopefully be a quick trip.

The front door opens, and I look up, expecting my mom. What I see is even better; Summer Swanson, my crush of two years. I sat behind her freshman year in English. I asked to borrow a pencil, and I swear, when her fingers brushed mine, I'd felt a spark. She's as beautiful now as she was that first day I saw her. Her long blonde hair shines under the fluorescent lights, framing her round face. The woman holding the door open for her must be her mom because they look so much alike.

My joy at seeing her is short lived when I see how pale she looks. Despite the California heat outside, she's clutching a sweater close to her body.

Her mom gives her a half-hug and sends her in my direction. I straighten up in my chair and drop the tissue in my lap, hoping the blood has quit dripping. I'm pretty sure my hair is a mess after my fall, and I attempt to finger comb it. Too late, I realize I'm probably smearing blood through it. I hope it blends into my brown hair. Maybe she'll just think I have red highlights.

Summer sits across from me, but doesn't spare a glance in my direction. She's staring at her hands, which are now balled into fists in her lap. She looks miserable, and I want to make her feel better.

I clear my throat, but she still doesn't look. I move closer, leaving one chair between us. I don't want to come on *too* strong.

"So," I say, casually. "What are you in for?"

This gets her attention. She looks at me, and I'm blown away. Her eyes are the palest, most beautiful blue I've ever seen. I don't remember them being this pretty during our pencil exchange. I've seen her since, of course, at school, but never this close up.

"What?" she asks. The confused expression on her face might be the cutest thing I've ever seen.

I gesture to my own arm. "I'm in for a broken wrist. There was an incident with a skate rail." She raises her eyebrows, and I quickly add, "But you should see the rail—*way* worse off than me." This earns me a slight smile. "What about you?"

She shrugs and averts her gaze to her lap.

"Top secret?" I look around conspiratorially. "Don't worry, you don't have to tell me. I'll just assume it's worse than it actually is."

"Fever," she says. She's still trying to suppress a smile; I can see it tugging at the corners of her lips.

I lean back, away from her. "Hey, I've already got a broken bone. Are you trying to get me sick, too?"

"You are so weird."

"I prefer adorable, but I'll take what I can get." I flash her my most charming grin. "I'm Kane."

I have no doubt she's forgotten me and the pencil exchange. I never did work up the courage to talk to her again. She was always occupied with her friends, and I wasn't even a blip on her radar.

She does smile this time, for real, and it's like someone turned on the sun.

"Summer."

"My favorite season."

"Original."

I pretend her words hurt and clutch my good arm to my chest. "You mean you've heard that one before?"

Summer shrugs. "Only once or twice."

"I'll do better next time."

"What makes you think there will be a next time?"

"Because I like you Summer, and I think you like me too."

She rolls her eyes, then points to my face. "You're dripping blood."

I grab the tissue from my lap and try to catch the next drip. I don't know why I bother. I've already got blood down the front of my shirt. Hopefully Mom can clean that out, or at least find me another one. I love this shirt, though apparently, it's not as lucky as I'd hoped.

Mom, with impeccably bad timing, barges through the doors. She strides directly toward me and pauses a few feet away. Looking me up and down, she shakes her head. "Really, Kane?" Her tone is less annoyed than incredulous.

I grin. "Hey, at least it's not my dominant hand."

"Give me the clipboard." She holds out her hand, and I point to it, still on the seat where Mark left it. Mom sits across from me and gets to work.

While Mom is scribbling out my medical history, I turn my attention back to Summer. "So, where were we?"

"Kane Dwyer?" A nurse—I recognize her as Claudia Diaz—stands at the door leading back to the exam room. She's looking at me expectantly, and I groan. I'm surrounded by women with terrible timing today.

"I think you were about to get called into the exam room," Summer says, humor coloring her voice.

"Can I get your number?" I ask. It can't be chance that I've run into her here.

It's fate.

"Come on, Kane," Mom says, standing. She adjusts her purse on her shoulder, still scribbling information on the clipboard.

I turn to face her and hold up one finger on my good hand. I have to remove the tissue to do this, and I can feel blood dribbling down my chin. "One sec, Mom."

She gives me her "Mom" look. I know that look well. It means she has no time for my BS.

I grab my skateboard from the chair and reluctantly turn back to Summer. While walking backward, I say, "I'll see you at school."

"You don't know which school I go to."

I grin. "Unless you've transferred this year, we've been at the same school since freshman year. I'll keep my eyes peeled for you in the halls."

"Kane, turn around," Mom says. "Before you fall down and break your other arm."

I wink at Summer, who's still looking at me dumbfounded, and turn my back on her.

"Mom, it's my wrist," I say, as I follow her through the door Claudia is still holding open. "And you're *killing* my game."

"You're lucky your *'game'* is all I'm killing."

I trudge down the hall after her and into an exam room. Claudia takes my vitals, then leaves us to wait for the doctor. I spend the wait time listening to Mom lecture me about making better decisions and *blah blah blah*. I've heard it all before. It's kind of funny that she seems to think this time it will sink in. It's not like I *tried* to break my wrist. I just really wanted to nail the rail grind.

Finally, the doctor comes in. After stitching up my chin, he examines my arm. He takes some x-rays and confirms what I already know—I have indeed fractured my wrist. I could have told him that, but I keep my mouth shut. He sets the bone—which hurts like a bitch—and wraps it. Then he gives Mom a referral for an orthopedic surgeon to put a cast on.

Summer is no longer in the waiting area when the doctor finishes with me. She must be in another room, which is good for her and bad for me. I was hoping to see her one more time and convince her to give me her number. At least she knows I exist now.

As we exit the building, Mom reaches over and snatches my skateboard from my good hand.

"Mom!" I protest.

She gives me *The Look*, and says, "Until further notice, this is mine."

I don't want to push her too far, so I pause and think before I speak. "Any idea when that will be?"

She narrows her eyes. "At *least* until the cast comes off. You may not survive another injury, if you catch my drift." She cocks a brow at me, and I know she's mostly kidding.

"Fine," I grudgingly agree.

When we get to the car, she throws my skateboard in the back, and I group text Mark and Abigail.

KANE: My trip to UC was life changing.

MARK: Do I even want to know?

ABIGAIL: ???

KANE: I ran into the girl of my dreams.

MARK: Not literally, I hope.

KANE: Shut up.

2

SUMMER

Mom brings the car to a halt at a stop sign, and I stare across the stretch of golden beach outside my window. Beyond the long row of parking spaces and past the boardwalk, my old volleyball team is at the nets. Just before Mom pulls forward, I see Michelle Carver spike the ball into the sand on the opposite side. The girls on her side of the net high five each other, jumping up and down in celebration. My ex-best friend, Rachel Yang, is among them.

I miss being a part of the team.

Four months ago was the beginning of the end for me. That was when I got really sick. It started with aching in my joints, but my parents assured me it was probably growing pains. But soon I had a gross, scaly rash on my face, which I hid from *everyone,* including my parents, under a ton of concealer and foundation. Finally, I ended up with mono. When the doctors heard about all of my aches and pains, saw my rash, and ran numerous blood tests, I was diagnosed with lupus, a lifelong autoimmune disease. Now the sun is my enemy, too much time under the hot rays will cause my disease to flare up, so I had to quit volleyball.

After my diagnosis, I came across The Spoon Theory on the

internet. Healthy people start the day with a seemingly infinite number of "spoons." People with a chronic illness, like me, have a limited number, and that number varies from day to day. Every action takes a spoon. Something as simple as getting out of bed in the morning takes a spoon. Once you run out of spoons, you're screwed for the day, or sometimes longer. So, as much as I want to play volleyball, even if I could withstand the sun, I just don't have the spoons to spare right now.

I'm lucky that today's trip to urgent care was a false alarm. My usual low-grade fever spiked a little higher than normal. Mom freaked and took me in. The doctor advised Tylenol to bring down the fever and scheduling an appointment for blood work with my regular physician. The one who knows my case. So now I have more doctors and blood draws to look forward to. Like I don't see them enough already.

"So," Mom says, breaking the silence. "Who was that boy I saw you talking with in the waiting room?"

I glance at her out of the corner of my eye and see the knowing smile on her lips. Before I can stop myself, I roll my eyes. "I don't know. Some guy."

"Some guy?" Mom asks. It's clear from her tone of voice that she expects me to elaborate.

I shrug, fixing my gaze out the window again now that we've passed the beach.

Mom sighs, a sound I know all too well. She's giving up on trying to engage me in conversation for the time being. I'm grateful. I don't want to talk about that guy or anything else. But I know it won't be the end. Mom thinks it would be healthy for me to move on with another boyfriend. She has no clue that I dumped my last one, Bradley, after I found out he and Rachel kissed last spring at Prom.

We finally pull into the driveway, and the moment the wheels stop, I jump out of the car and hurry to my bedroom.

As soon as my bedroom door closes behind me, I hear excited footsteps racing down the hall. "Mom! Mom!" my sister, Mandy, yells. "I finally beat the level!" Oh, to be eleven and healthy again.

I switch on my music to drown out her voice and sit at my vanity, scrutinizing my reflection in the mirror. I turn my face this way and that, looking for any sign that my makeup is wearing off. I dab on more concealer, hiding any trace of the most obvious sign of my lupus; the purplish butterfly rash across both cheeks.

Satisfied that the evidence of my disease is hidden, I turn to my bookshelf and pull out last year's yearbook. The guy from urgent care recognized me from school, but I don't remember him. My high school isn't huge, how could I not recognize someone with whom I've shared a building for two years?

Flipping to last year's sophomore class, I page through, skimming the list of names for Kane. It doesn't take long before I find *Dwyer, Kane*. He's the only Kane at Sol del Mar High.

I shake my head. His hair was different last year, but I still don't recognize him. Flipping to the index in the back, I look to see if he was in any sports or clubs, but he wasn't. His only appearance in the yearbook is his school headshot. It shouldn't bother me that I don't remember him, but it does.

I close the book and return it to the shelf. Laying on my bed, I realize that this year's yearbook will only feature one photo of me. I've always been active in clubs and sports. Volleyball, debate, show choir...the list went on. Knowing that I won't be on those pages is like my disease pointing a finger at me and laughing.

I didn't have to quit all of my activities, but the thought of letting down any of my teammates makes me too anxious. Better to hide out alone, at home, than disappoint them.

I roll over, turning my back on the bookshelf in annoyance, and try to nap.

It feels like only seconds have passed when Mandy bursts into my room and I'm jolted awake. She jumps on the end of my bed chanting, "Dinner! Dinner! Dinner!"

I try to shoo her from my room, but eleven-year-olds aren't the most compliant of people. Finally, I give up and let her drag me by the hand to the dinner table.

Mom is standing over the crockpot, poking at a pork loin. "Summer, dishes. Mandy, silverware. Please and thank you."

She's very efficient in her orders, and we do as we're told. I set a plate for each of us at the table and glare at the pills waiting for me when I reach my spot.

My drug cocktail varies between appointments with my doctors. Currently I'm on azathioprine for my aching joints; hydroxychloroquine for my skin and arthritis; and prednisone, a steroid that helps prevent my body from attacking itself. Combined, my pills have a mile long list of side effects, including; nausea, tiredness, loss of appetite, headaches, and an increased chance of skin cancer.

Mandy takes her seat across from me, and I gather up my meds. I swallow them with a large gulp of water from the cup already waiting for me at the table.

"No Dad tonight?" I ask, glancing at his empty seat.

"You know your father," Mom says, shaking her head. "Working late on an important case."

My parents are both lawyers, but Mom is real estate and Dad is criminal law. He's always working late on a case.

Mom sets the pork loin on the table, and Mandy scrunches up her nose in disgust. "I'm not eating that." Her voice is matter of fact, and she crosses her arms over her chest and gives her blonde head a defiant shake.

Mom stares at her. "You love pork loin."

"Mom even made it with bacon on top," I add, gesturing to the platter.

"Do you even *know* where pork and bacon *come from*?"

Mandy demands, her mouth agape in horror as her brown eyes shift between Mom and me.

After exchanging a look with me, Mom slowly says, "Yes..."

Mandy's eyes grow wide. "You knew all this time that we were eating cute little pigs?"

"It's the circle of life, Amanda," Mom says, though she doesn't roll her eyes, I can hear it in her voice. She's using Mandy's full name; she wants to end this ASAP. "And they're not *little* pigs."

"I don't care. I'm not eating that. I'm a vegetarian now."

I squeeze my eyes shut. I think I'm getting a headache, and I don't think my lupus is to blame. When I open them again, Mom's lips are a tight line, and she's engaged in a staring contest with my sister. Mom blinks first, and says, "Then you'll just have to fill up on green beans."

Mandy scowls. "I *hate* green beans."

"Too bad."

Mom begins dishing pork onto her own plate, followed by a healthy spoonful of steamed green beans. They look disgusting, and I eye up Mandy, who is also watching Mom. I wonder if she'll cave and eat the pork.

I take the serving fork and place a piece of meat onto my own plate. Then I add a significantly smaller serving of green beans than Mom took. Like Mandy, I also hate green beans, but Mom won't let me leave the table if I don't eat at least a few. Then it's Mandy's turn. I bring a bite of pork to my lips and watch her carefully; she's still glaring at the dish of limp and soggy vegetables. Finally, she reaches out and fills her plate. She grimaces with every bite she takes, but she clears her plate in record time and then asks to be excused.

"Wow," I say, once Mandy has loaded her plate into the dishwasher and left the room.

"How long do you think this will last?" Mom asks, a hint of despair in her voice.

"I honestly thought she'd cave when you said she had to eat the green beans."

"So did I."

We sit in silence for a moment, then Mom says, "Are you looking forward to seeing your friends at school?"

I shrug. School starts in two weeks, and I've avoided everyone all summer. They quit calling after the first couple weeks, so I guess I wasn't that important to them anyway.

"I worry about you, Sweetie. I want to see you hanging out with friends again, okay?"

I push my food around my plate and nod. Great, now I need to make excuses to not come home after school and lie about still having friends.

"Anyway," Mom says, changing the subject. "I thought we'd go school supply shopping tomorrow when I get home from work."

I shrug. "You have the list. You can just get me whatever I need. I don't really care."

Mom frowns but doesn't say anything. I've always insisted on going with for school supplies to make sure Mom didn't buy the ugly colored folders or the wrong brand of pencils. But it's hard to care about things like that once you find out you'll be sick for the rest of your life.

As soon as I excuse myself from the dinner table, I return to my bedroom and pull out my sketch pad and pencil. Since I stopped spending time around people, I've taken up sketching. I used to draw all the time when I was Mandy's age, but stopped when homework and friends and my clubs and activities took over. Now, it's the only thing that gives me any semblance of joy.

Flipping to a clean page, I sketch the outline of a wave on the ocean and get lost in my art.

3

KANE

Never before have I been so anxious for the school year to begin. It's been two weeks since I broke my wrist. Two *agonizingly long* weeks not only without my skateboard, but also without running into Summer again. I was sure it was fate that brought us to the urgent care waiting room at the same time, but with each day that passes, I doubt fate more. But today's the first day of junior year, and I *know* she'll be here.

Pedaling into the school lot, I narrowly avoid turning in front of a blue Ford Focus. I raise one hand at the driver in a "my bad" gesture then roll my bike to a stop on the sidewalk, chaining it to the bike rack next to a few others.

The California sun is already shining at seven in the morning, and I know it's gonna be one of the hotter ones. I've dressed for the heat in a pair of cargo shorts and a t-shirt that says, "Tacosaurus." It's green and has a picture of a taco shaped like a stegosaurus.

Any other first day of school, I'd be annoyed at being cooped indoors all day when I could be outside skating or biking. But this year is different; Summer knows I exist. Assuming she remembers me from our all too brief conversation.

Watching Mark and Abigail skate, and surf, and do all the cool stuff I've been banned from doing has sucked. But I've honored Mom's wishes and played it safe. I've managed to stay free of any new injuries. Well, major injuries anyway.

The only thing that's gotten me through is Mom letting me keep my bike. Under the condition that I use it for its intended purpose and not for stunts.

Not seeing my friends yet, I text Mark and Abigail. Abigail texts back right away, letting me know they've just parked and will meet me by the bike racks.

I hop up, seating myself on the metal rack. Balancing on the bar, I scan the crowd of students. Every blonde girl I see has me looking twice, but none of them are Summer. I'm beginning to think she's transferred to another school when my friends approach.

I know, it's a little crazy to be fixated on this girl I talked to for all of five minutes over the course of two years, but I can't remember the last time a girl smiled at me like she had. Excluding my mom—for obvious reasons—and Abigail, because she's like a sister to me.

"Aww, Mark, look how cute Kane is." Abigail reaches up to rub my head, and I swat her away with my good arm. Losing my balance, I fall off the bike rack. Somehow, I manage to not fall on my ass when I stumble and regain my footing.

Mark laughs and shakes his head. I glare, but it's halfhearted.

"Have you spotted her yet?" Abigail asks, taking my vacated seat on the metal rail.

"Would I be standing here if I had?"

Abigail shrugs and pushes her red bangs out of her eyes. "What's she look like again? We'll help look."

I shrug helplessly. "Can mere words be used to describe an angel?"

Mark laughs so hard he snorts, and I elbow him in the ribs.

"Okay, but really," Mark says, recovering from his fit of laughter and my elbow. "At least give us a hair color to go on."

"Blonde," I say and return my attention to the students streaming past us.

"Gee. A blonde girl in Southern California." I can hear the sarcasm in Mark's voice but choose to ignore it.

"Well, as fun as it is helping Kane stalk this poor girl, I think it's time to head in. I don't want to be late on the first day." Abigail hops off the bike rack—far more gracefully than I had—and strides toward the school's front doors. Despite looking like someone who couldn't care less about school, with her dark eye makeup and the line of piercings running up her ears, Abigail has the best grades of our trio.

"Come on, Kane, you have all year to find her." Mark jogs away to catch up to Abigail.

I give one last fleeting look around, then follow my friends into the school.

By the time my lunch period comes around, I've pretty much given up on seeing Summer again. I'm half-convinced that in the pain-induced delirium from my fractured wrist I may have imagined her.

The best part of school is eating lunch outside. There are plenty of tables in the cafeteria, but my friends and I have always preferred eating in the courtyard.

I find Mark at the same table we sat at last year, in the shade of the only oak tree in the outdoor eating space.

"So?" he asks.

"So what?"

"Did you find her?"

I shake my head, glum and defeated. "Maybe fate isn't on my side after all."

Mark doesn't reply, his mouth is full of cafeteria quesadilla.

I scan our surroundings. The courtyard looks the same as

always, a dozen or so rectangular picnic tables slowly filling with other students as they exit the cafeteria doors with lunch trays in hand.

And then I see her.

As my gaze shifts to the cafeteria door, Summer comes striding through. She has on a long-sleeved purple top, and her hair is loose around her shoulders. She finds an empty table in the shade of the building and sets down a blue lunch box. I think it has purple butterflies on the side, but I can't tell from this far away.

I realize I've frozen in place when I feel Mark kick me under the table. "Earth to Kane."

I jerk my head in Summer's direction and say, "It's her."

Mark cocks an eyebrow and glances between Summer and me.

"Bye." I grin at Mark and take one moment to quick finger comb my hair, then I gather up my things, stand, and march up to her table. I sit down across from her and pull a brown bag lunch from my backpack.

She looks up in surprise. I half-expect her to tell me to go away, but she just stares at me.

I take my PB&J out of the plastic sandwich keeper and take a bite. I swallow and grin at her.

"Hi, Summer, I'm sure you remember me from urgent care." When she doesn't say anything, my smile falters. "Kane?"

"I remember you," she says quietly. She's dipping a carrot stick in a little container of dip over and over again, but she doesn't take a bite. She's not the same Summer I remember from the last two years. That Summer would be in the cafeteria, talking and laughing with her friends.

I ignore the oddity of her sitting out here alone and let out a relieved breath. "Good. That will make this easier."

She stares at me in confusion, a cute little crease forming between her eyes, but she doesn't say anything.

Here goes nothing. I play it cool and say the words I've been rehearsing in my head for the past two weeks. "I'd like to ask you out, Summer." I take another bite of my sandwich, chew, swallow, and grin at her again.

Her mouth falls open, and the hand dipping the carrot stills. "You don't even know me."

It's not a no.

"Exactly," I say. I pull out a juice pouch and poke the straw through the foil packaging. "But I'd like to. What do you say? You and me, dinner and a movie Friday night?"

She shakes her head. "I can't."

I'd be lying if I said I'm not disappointed by her response, but I'm not taking no for an answer. I've spent way too much time planning out what I was going to say when I saw her again, and what we would do when I got her to go out with me. When I set my mind to something I don't back down, which is why they know me so well at the urgent care.

"Okay, not Friday. What about Saturday?"

She shakes her head again, and there's a sinking feeling in the pit of my stomach. "I'm flattered, Kane, really, but..." Her eyes bore holes into the table between us.

"But what? I'm not your type?" I've heard that one before. But none of those rejections stung like this, because none of those girls were Summer.

Her lips curve up into a little smile. Just as quickly, it's gone. She shakes her head again. "I'm not at a place in my life where I can date right now. I'm sorry."

I sigh. *This* is a rejection I *haven't* heard before.

"You seem really nice," she adds quickly.

"Will you at least sign my cast?" I hold my injured arm toward her.

She hesitates, then nods. "Okay."

I dig around in my backpack. Finally, I fish a marker out from beneath my math and English textbooks and hand it to her. I slide my arm across the table and hope the cast doesn't repel her. I'm a teenager and guy; that's a messy combination. After two weeks, my cast is looking pretty grimy and is no longer the vibrant blue it once was.

Summer's eyes scan the cast before she settles on a place to sign. Her palm brushes my fingertips, and I grin at the contact. Her hands are soft, but her fingers are surprisingly cold. I want to tell her I'll warm them up, but I bite it back. I don't want to scare her off.

In beautiful, loopy cursive, she scrawls her name across the cast. She returns the marker and her phone begins chirping. Pulling it out of her bag, she silences it.

"Sorry, I've got to go." She closes her container of dip. Quickly stuffing the remains of her lunch into her bag, she slings it over one arm and flees toward the school.

I'm left alone, rejected, and blinking in confusion. Finally, I call after her, "See ya later!"

Disappointed, I slowly stuff my lunch back in the brown bag, then trudge over to my usual table. Abigail has joined Mark, and I sit down across from her.

"So, that was Summer, huh?" Abigail says. She wiggles her eyebrows suggestively. "She's cute."

I glare. "She's more than cute, she's beautiful," I say. "And I already called dibs."

"Dibs don't count if she bats for my team and not yours." Abigail laughs, then takes a bite of her quesadilla.

"So, did you ask her out?" Mark asks.

"I did," I answer without elaborating. Maybe they won't ask for details.

"And..." Abigail prompts, waving her hands in the air.

"I'm working on it," I mumble.

Mark laughs. "She turned you down. Sorry, buddy."

"She didn't turn me down..." I sigh and throw up my arms.

"Okay, she turned me down. But it wasn't a *hard no*," I insist, looking pointedly between both my friends. "It was more of an, 'I'm-not-dating-right-now' kind of rejection. I think I can change her mind." I nod, determined.

Mark and Abigail exchange a look, and I can tell they don't believe me. This just fuels my determination to win Summer over. There's something going on with her, she seems sad, and I want to be the one to cheer her up.

4

SUMMER

S aved by the bell, or rather, the alarm on my phone. I hurry
into the school building—away from Kane—and through the
halls until I reach the nurse's office. Miss Hill, the school nurse,
greets me with a smile. Her dark eyes sparkle with warmth.

"Did you have a good break, Summer?"

Miss Hill is only twenty-five, so it's easier to talk to her than
some of the other adults. Today, her curly black hair is pulled back
with a thick brown headband, and she's wearing her trademark
shade of MAC lipstick; Antique Velvet. It looks amazing against
her rich brown skin, but awful next to my own warm ivory pallor.

Toward the end of last school year, I'd gotten to know Miss Hill
well. I spent a lot of time in her office before and after my
diagnosis.

I shrug. "It was fine. How was yours."

Nurse Hill beams and holds her left hand out for me to see.
Her nails are painted a gorgeous shade of crimson, but it's the
diamond sparkling from a gold band that catches my eye.

"Wow. Sean popped the question?"

She nods in excitement. "Last month. We're planning the
wedding for next summer."

"That's great," I say. "I'm really happy for you."

"Thanks."

Taking a seat in the plastic chair next to her desk, I hug my backpack in my lap. Miss Hill unlocks the medicine cabinet and retrieves my meds. I fiddle with one of the gold and turquoise beaded bracelets adorning my left wrist.

There's a photograph on the desk beside me and I inspect it while I wait. Nurse Hill with her new fiancé. I frown, jealous of her normal life. I'll never have a fiancé, because I'll never curse anyone to a life of having to deal with me and my illness.

She turns back to me, a plastic bag of pill bottles in hand, and frowns. "You okay?" she asks.

I nod and force a smile. I don't think she buys it, but she doesn't say anything.

While she counts out the pills, I pull a bottle of water from my backpack. She watches as I swallow each one and drain the bottle.

"Looks like your dosage of Prednisone has gone down since I last saw you in the spring," she says. Her voice is optimistic and chipper; exactly the opposite of how I've felt every second since my diagnosis.

"Yep." I don't tell her that I've been on and off the stuff all summer, at various dosages.

"Well, off to class with you then. Lunch ends in—" Nurse Hill glances at the clock on the wall, "—three minutes." She turns her back on me to lock up my medications, and I grab my bag and walk to the door.

"Hey, Summer?" she calls.

I freeze with my hand on the door handle and turn back and meet her eye.

"If you need anything, even just to talk, come see me, okay? I'm a good listener."

I nod, and Miss Hill flashes that warm smile of hers again.

Yeah, right, like talking would help. I'm broken, and there is no cure. I'll be on medications for the rest of my life, until one by one my organs fail, and nothing can help me anymore.

Leaving the office, the halls are nearly empty. I'm almost to my next classroom when the bell rings. Students stream out of the cafeteria, and I'm thrown back into the everyday chaos of high school. I'm surrounded by my peers who are healthy and happy, their entire lives ahead of them. I feel a surge of anger and resentment bubble up. Last year, I was just like them. My only worries in the world were getting my homework in on time and what to wear to prom.

"Hi, Summer."

I turn at my name and come face to face with my ex-best friend.

"Hey," I mumble, hoping she can hear how unenthused I am at her presence.

"How's it going?" Rachel looks around at our classmates streaming past. She's clearly as uncomfortable with this conversation as I am. I wonder why she's even instigating it. After she cheated with my boyfriend, I was so hurt and angry, I dumped them both and haven't spoken to either since. I lost nine years of friendship with that one kiss.

"I'm fine," I answer. As the words spew from my mouth, I realize how clipped they sound. It's a lie, of course, but one I've been telling so people will leave me alone and not ask more questions. It's not like they *actually* want to know how I am. If I tell the truth, I'll just scare them away, so I force a smile to alleviate some of the tension.

"Oh, okay, good." Rachel doesn't look like she believes me, but I don't really care. "So...you really quit the Volleyball team."

I nod. "I'm focusing on classes this year." More lies. It took all summer to get my medications straightened out, and it quickly became apparent that volleyball took too many spoons. I love it, and I miss it, but I've come to accept that it's a part of my past now.

"That's good," she replies. Her gaze wanders around the hall again, as if searching for an escape. But she keeps talking. "I hoped it wasn't because...because of me."

For a split second, I consider telling her that it *is* her fault I quit. But even if that were true, I wouldn't want to let her know she had that much power over me. Instead, I force a laugh, and hope it doesn't sound as fake to her as it does to my own ears.

"Of course not." Then I give us both an out from this awkward conversation. "But I've got to run if I'm going to get to class on time."

"Oh, yeah, right. No problem. I'll see you later."

I give her a terse smile and hurry down the hall and around the corner until I reach the girls restroom. I walk to the row of sinks and stare at my reflection in the mirror, checking to make sure my rash is still hidden.

Satisfied my disguise is still in place, I head to my foods class. It's an elective where we learn about food from different cultures around the world. It seemed like an easy A.

Entering the classroom, I look around for a friendly and familiar face to sit by. Or better yet, an empty seat away from anyone else. The classroom is set up with two rows of tables, each seating two students, and a path down the middle.

With less than a minute left until the tardy bell rings, there are only two vacant seats, and I have to decide fast. The first is beside Rachel. After what she did at prom, I don't think I can tolerate an entire term in such close proximity.

The second seat is by Kane. Why is this guy suddenly every-where? I've been wracking my brain, and I swear I've never seen him before. He has another dorky t-shirt on today, this one with a taco dinosaur. He's kind of cute though, with his basic boy haircut and friendly brown eyes. Every time he speaks to me he has a grin on his face and his eyes light up. He oozes confidence, which is both super attractive and intimidating. What teenager has that much confidence? It's unnatural.

It doesn't take long to decide. With more confidence than I feel, I stride to the chair beside Kane and sit down. He looks over and his eyes light up.

"Hey," he says. He doesn't bother trying to hide his smile. Other guys would, in some attempt to appear cool, but not Kane. It's that confidence thing again. He doesn't cover up his feelings, he's happy right now and not afraid to let the world know.

"Hey," I say back, setting my bag on the floor beside me.

Our teacher, Ms. Knope, calls the class to order and takes attendance.

"Turn to your table mate," Ms. Knope announces from the front of the room. "And say hello to your partner for the remainder of the term."

"You know..." He chews on the end of his pen thoughtfully. "This isn't dinner and a movie, but sitting next to you in class every day for the next couple months might be even better."

I stare at my hands folded on the table in front of me and suppress a groan.

On my way to choir, I see Mr. Kaiser taping a sheet of paper up on the wall near the auditorium door. He teaches English and is also head of the drama department. Before I can get close enough to see what it is, Rachel rounds the corner and rushes to the sheet. A smile appears on her face and she snatches the pen, which is dangling from a piece of yarn taped to the wall, and quickly scrawls across the paper. I wait until she's disappeared into the choir room before I approach.

Fall Play Sign Ups

I stare at the words on the sheet. It's exactly what I expected. The date for auditions is set for two weeks from now, but beneath that is a place to sign up for stage crew. I see Rachel's name. Every year she and I have done backstage work for the school plays. Costumes and makeup.

Not this year.

Rachel and my disease have taken this from me too.

Turning my back on the signup sheet, I enter the choir room and take the seat I had last year. I'm a second soprano. Thankfully, Rachel is an alto, so she's on the other side of the room. I don't have to speak to her the entire period while Ms. Hammond goes through and listens to each of us sing. Afterward, she assigns us new seats for the year. I shift one seat to the right, which is one seat further away from the altos and fine by me. I don't look at Rachel to see if she's moved. I'm pretty sure I feel her eyes on me though.

Before choir ends, Ms. Hammond tells us she'll be holding auditions for the show choir on Friday. Another activity I'm losing.

As soon as the bell rings, I rush out of the room before Rachel has a chance to ambush me again. When I get to my math class, I'm happy to see that, though I recognize most of the faces, none belong to any of my former friends. I take a seat in the back corner and pretend to be invisible. This day can't end soon enough.

5

———

KANE

The sound of polyurethane wheels on concrete is music to my ears. The only thing that makes it sweeter is when those wheels are attached to my own board beneath my feet.

My board is still locked up though, and I'm itching to get back out there. Instead, I keep my butt firmly planted on the sidelines. Watching everyone else have all the fun. Mom would be so proud.

Mark and Abigail skate over and dismount their boards. Mark grabs their water bottles from beside me and hands Abigail hers.

School has been out for almost an hour, and on the drive to the skatepark I told them all about my class with Summer.

"Okay, so you have a class with her, now what?" Abigail asks before taking a long drink from her bottle.

"Now I get her to fall in love with me." Isn't that obvious?

Mark snorts, and I ignore him. He's just jealous because he's single and miserable. Okay, he's not miserable. Mark seems content with Abigail, me, and his surfboard. He spends so much time surfing, I'm pretty sure he doesn't have time for a girlfriend.

"You're adorable, Kane," Abigail says. She reaches out to pat my head, and I slap her hand away. I'm not sure why she's always trying to mess with my hair, but it drives me crazy. Actually, that's *probably* why she's always trying to mess with my hair.

"Has she even said more than five words to you?" Mark asks.

I pause to consider. "Yes. She's definitely said more than five words to me. Possibly even ten or fifteen."

"Have you considered that she might not be interested?" Mark insists.

"I refuse to let your negativity burst my bubble."

The skin under my cast is beginning to itch. I dig a pen out of my backpack and push it under the cast as far as I can, trying to reach the spot.

"*Please* tell me you didn't do *that* in front of her," Abigail says. When I look up, she's cringing.

"What? It itches."

Mark snorts again. "Kane. A regular Romeo."

"I need to find out what she likes. I'm sure we have *something* in common."

I'm actually *not* sure. She doesn't seem like she's the kind of girl to skate, or BMX, or even surf. I really don't know anything about her, except that she was in the show choir last year, and she plays volleyball. I attended every choir concert and volleyball game just to feast my eyes on her. And, oh yeah, she's the prettiest girl at Sol del Mar High. It's not much to base a relationship on, but hey, you've got to start somewhere, right?

"Tomorrow, I'm going to find out everything there is to know about her." I give my friends a determined nod.

Abigail slips a stick of gum in her mouth and chews. She blows a bubble and lets it pop. "That's a tall order for a fifty minute class."

After yesterday's failure to win over Summer, I'm eager to see her at lunch and try again. But she's not here. I sit with Mark and Abigail, but spend the time half listening to their conversation while I keep my eyes peeled for her to appear. I'm afraid she won't be in foods class, but fortunately I'm wrong. When I arrive, she's already seated at our table, her arms crossed on the surface with her head resting on them.

"Hey, Sleeping Beauty," I say softly as I take my seat beside her. I don't want to startle her.

She sits upright and looks at me in surprise. "Oh, hey."

It isn't the friendliest of welcomes, but it isn't *un*welcoming either.

"How's it going?" I ask, setting my bag on the floor beside me. I catch a light scent of coconut wafting off her skin.

She shrugs. "Another day in paradise."

I grin. With her beside me, it *is* paradise.

"So, I've been thinking," I say. She arches a brow and watches me skeptically. "I really don't know anything about you, besides the fact that you enjoy hanging out in the urgent care as much as I do."

She casts a glance around the room, as if making sure nobody heard me, then raises her brow again.

"I'm glad you seem to be over that fever." I wink to show her I'm just playing. "So anyway, I have a list of questions to ask you. Are you game?"

"Why?" she asks.

I blink, confused by her question. "Why what?"

She shakes her head and frowns. I hate seeing that frown on her face. "Why do you want to know me?"

I laugh. "Why *wouldn't* I want to know you?"

She still looks confused.

I pull a notebook out of my bag and dramatically clear my throat. In an exaggerated game show host voice, I read from the list I've prepared. "First question. What is your favorite color?"

She smiles for real this time, and it lights up the room. For a moment, I don't think she'll answer, but finally she says, "Blue."

"Ahh," I say. "I pegged you for a pink kind of girl."

"Why?"

I shrug. "I don't know. Don't all girls like pink?"

Her smile turns into a grin. "Do all boys like video games?"

I pretend to look shocked. "Of course they do. What kind of question is *that*?"

She shakes her head, but the smile remains. "Well, not *all* girls like pink."

"For the record, blue is also *my* favorite color. Moving on. Pizza or tacos?"

"Tacos. Then pizza. Or maybe taco pizza?"

"Seriously? It's like we're the same person. I think we might be soulmates."

Before I can move on to the third question on my list, Ms. Knope calls the class to order. I wink at Summer and try to focus on the lesson.

Over the next week and a half, I bombard Summer with questions before class starts. She keeps relatively quiet while I talk at her, usually giving one word answers—probably just to shut me up. But every once in a while she catches me by surprise and engages me in conversation.

I've noticed she keeps to herself and doesn't smile much these days, not like she used to. But when I talk to her, the corners of her lips twitch upward. Though she rarely says much, those tiny almost smiles give me hope. And the infrequent real ones make my heart race and my palms get sweaty. I live for those real smiles.

She's so reserved this year, and I have no clue why, but I think she's starting to warm up to me. As much as I want to spend time with her for my own selfish reasons, I think I might be good for her too.

I finally decide I need to step up my game. I'm no longer satisfied with these few minutes before class and while Ms. Knope isn't looking. I need to take a leap, especially since homecoming is coming up. I've seen posters appearing in the halls. White and turquoise poster board covered in paint and glitter, reminding us of the big game and dance. I want Summer to be my date.

"What are you doing after school?" I ask by way of greeting, taking my seat beside her. Summer is busy doodling something in her notebook.

She shrugs, her eyes not leaving the paper. "Nothing, I guess."

"Great. Why don't we hang out and get to know each other better?"

She hesitates, then says, "What did you have in mind?"

"Meet me by the bike rack after school."

Her pencil pauses, then her eyes meet mine. She chews her lower lip and I hold my breath, fingers crossed under the table, willing her to say yes. It feels like an eternity before she finally says, "Sure."

I'm semi-shocked, but mostly excited that she's just agreed to spend time with me outside of class. The grin on my face is so big it actually hurts. She's wearing a small smile of her own, though she's trying to hide it from me.

The rest of the school day drags, as I count down the minutes until I'll see her again. When the final bell rings, I charge toward the exit, not caring who I bump into in my mad dash for the bike rack. I'm afraid that if Summer arrives first and I'm not there, she'll leave. I can't miss this opportunity. I need to know her.

Panting, I skid to a stop at the rack. I put my hands on the top bar and lean forward, catching my breath. I've nearly recovered when I hear, "Do you always race through the halls like that?"

I stand up straight and turn around to find Summer walking toward me. She's smiling, and I grin back.

"You made it," I say.

"I said I'd be here, didn't I?"

"People say a lot of things."

"So, where to?" she asks, looking around.

I move to the other side of the bike rack and begin twisting in the code to unlock the chain. "You ready to go for a ride?"

"Wait, what?" Summer's eyes grow wide, and she takes a step back, her grip on her backpack tightening.

"It's not far. I promise it's safe."

"Was whatever you did to break your wrist safe?"

I wave my non-casted hand away. "That was different. Come on." I pull the bike from the rack, and once the tires are flat on the pavement, I mount up and pat the handlebars.

"I can't believe I'm doing this," she mutters. But she slips her arms through her backpack straps so that it's on her front and climbs on the handlebars. This is another point for her in my book.

"If you crash and injure me, I *will* kill you."

I smile at her threat. She doesn't have to worry; I'll be a lot more careful with her on the bike than if I was on my own. No fancy tricks or speedy trips down hills. Just point A to point B, safe and sound. Contrary to what my mom and friends believe, I *am* capable of not taking risks. Sometimes.

Safe and—relatively—slow, I pedal the bike the few blocks to the skatepark. The breeze sends her coconut scent toward me, and it's stronger now than it ever is in class. When we arrive, I stop in front of the bike rack and steady the bike with my feet.

"This is it," I say.

Summer slides off the handlebars and looks around. She slips the backpack from her arms and slings it over one shoulder. "Um... what is this?"

"This is my skatepark."

"The scene of the crime?" she asks, eyeing my wrist.

I laugh and hold up my plaster cast like a trophy. "One and the same."

"So, why are we here?"

"I told you I wanted to get to know you, and I figure you'll be more willing to open up if you get to know me. So, I'm letting you in on all my secrets. And not-so-secrets. This is my favorite place."

She looks around again. She doesn't look impressed.

"I know it's not much. There are nicer places around to skate at, but this one is close to school and my house. Plus they sell the best carne asada fries at the Snack Shack."

"Okay, so, show me around then."

I pause to lock up my bike, then lead her through the entrance.

"Sup Dennis." He's sitting on the wall near the entrance arch, probably stoned, as usual.

Dennis reaches out and fist bumps me. "How long until your mom gives your board back?"

I groan. "Not soon enough." I hold up my left arm. "Hopefully when this thing comes off in a week or two."

"That sucks man. Why do you torture yourself coming here when you can't skate?"

"Because you'd miss me too much if I stayed away."

Dennis rolls his eyes. "Who's this?" His eyes travel up and down Summer's body, and I put my arm around her protectively. She doesn't shrug me off or punch me, so I take that as a good sign.

"This is Summer."

"Sup, Summer." Dennis winks at her. Actually *winks* at her!

I shoot him a glare.

Dennis is what my mom calls "classically handsome"—whatever that means. He has blond hair and blue eyes to go with his permanently tanned skin. Abigail says he should be a model, instead of sitting around the skatepark all day smoking weed.

"Um, hey..." Summer shifts her weight from foot to foot. She's clearly uncomfortable with the attention.

"See you later, Dennis." I steer Summer away from him and into the park.

"He seems...nice," she says.

"He is. Harmless too." I release my hold on her and spread my arms out to the sides. "Anyway, this is where the magic happens."

"You did *not* just say that." She gives me an incredulous look, but the corners of her mouth twitch up in a smile.

"Oh, but I did." I grin. Pointing across the park at one of the small ramps, I say, "That's where I split my lip in the fourth grade."

"Ouch." She cringes, her hand flying to her mouth. She's probably imagining a smaller version of me falling off a board, my face covered in blood.

"It wasn't so bad. I kept skating until my mom came to pick me up." I laugh. "She was pissed I didn't call her right away."

"So you kept skating with blood dripping down your face?"

I nod, still grinning.

"You're crazy."

"I only needed a couple of stitches."

Summer steps in front of me, studying my face, or rather, my mouth. I look at her own glossy pink lips, parted slightly as she examines my face, and I swallow.

"Ahh," she says. Then she reaches out, and with her pointer finger, touches my lower lip.

I freeze, while my heart begins to race.

"Right here?"

I nod. I've forgotten how to form words, let alone breathe.

Summer steps back, turning her attention to the park again. This girl is killing me. Does she even realize what she's doing to me?

I take a deep breath, clear my throat, and point to another ramp. "Over there is where I broke my wrist the first time."

She shakes her head. "You really are an Evel Knievel. Where did you break your wrist this time?"

I point to the skate rail, which is three and a half feet off the ground and slopes downward beside a set of concrete steps.

"Holy crap. You tried to skate on that thing?"

I nod and laugh. "I did for a while, but I celebrated too soon and lost my balance."

"How are you not constantly covered in bandages?"

"Believe it or not, sometimes he *doesn't* fall down," comes a female voice from behind us. I turn around to face the owner of the voice.

"Hey guys," I say. "This is Summer." I turn back to Summer. "Summer, these are my best friends, Mark and Abigail."

"Oh, hey, we have chemistry together, don't we?" Summer says to Mark.

"We do. I didn't know you were the girl Kane's been going on and on about."

I reach out and slap his arm. Mark laughs. I look back to Summer and see that she's smiling. Hopefully Mark hasn't scared her off.

"I was just giving Summer the grand tour," I explain.

"What does the grand tour consist of?" Abigail quirks an eyebrow and narrows her eyes.

"I think he's telling me about every injury he's sustained here," Summer says before I can answer.

Mark groans.

"This is going to be a long tour then," Abigail says dryly.

"Shut up. You guys are the worst best friends ever." I barrage them with a series of playful smacks on the arms.

My friends leave us to go skate, and I take Summer to the Snack Shack. I buy us a jumbo serving of carne asada fries, and we take a seat on the sidelines to eat while we watch Abigail and Mark.

"This is actually kind of cool," she says after a few minutes of watching my friends fly by on their boards, performing stunts on the low ramps and rails. "I've never really watched skateboarding before."

"You ready to get out there?" I tease, helping myself to a couple of fries piled high with meat, cheese, sour cream, and guacamole.

"Um, I think not." She gives me a look that makes me think she's questioning my sanity, and laughs.

"You're right. You'd better wait until I get my board back. I'll teach you."

"Learn from the guy who has more injuries than candles on his cake?"

"You can learn from my mistakes."

"Pass." She swipes a clean fry from the basket and dips it in the sour cream before taking a bite.

"We'll table this for now. But I'm not giving up. Someday I *will* get you out there on a board." She shakes her head, and I sigh. "All right, so you know about me, what do *you* like to do?"

"You'll laugh." Her cheeks flush pink, and she looks down, her hair falling forward and concealing her face.

"I promise I won't. Try me."

She tips her head back and stares at the clear blue sky. Groaning she says, "I was a beauty blogger."

I stare at her, trying to figure out what the hell a beauty blogger is.

"Okay, that look you're giving me might be worse than laughing."

I shake my head. "It's like you're speaking another language. What is a beauty blogger, and why would I laugh?" I scrunch my brow and stare at her, willing her to answer. I know what a blogger is, and I know beauty when I see it, but combined? I'm lost.

"I had a blog where I talked about makeup and hair and stuff."

"Oh." That's it? I don't get why she's making a big deal of it. "Why would I laugh at that?"

She shrugs. "I don't know. Because it's silly? And not cool like skateboarding." She gestures at Mark as he grinds down the same rail I broke my wrist on almost a month ago.

I laugh. "So what? Just because it's nothing like skateboarding doesn't mean it's not cool. I mean, if you like it, that makes it cool enough for me."

She smiles, and then I realize she's used the past tense.

"But wait, you said was. You don't do this beauty blogging thing anymore?"

She shook her head. "No...it's a long story. I don't want to get into it."

She bites her lip and looks everywhere but at me. I don't respond right away. Of course I want to know this long story. I want to know everything there is to know about her. "Can I read your blog sometime?"

"You want me to help you choose a mascara?"

I grin. "Sure. If it makes you happy."

She smiles but tries to hide it.

I decide to change the subject. "Tell me something else."

"Like what?"

"I don't know. Anything. Tell me something else you love."

"Volleyball," she says automatically.

"Okay, cool, I know what volleyball is." I beam at her. "You're on the school team, right?"

Her smile falters. "No, not anymore..."

She avoids eye contact, chewing her lip again. This girl is full of secrets, and I'm dying to uncover them.

"Let me guess, another really long story?"

She nods.

"Someday I'm going to get you to spill."

6

SUMMER

Kane is charming.

But I'm not a princess, and my disease isn't a dragon some prince can slay. I'm a ticking time bomb and getting close to people will only hurt them. So, as charming as Kane is, I should keep pushing him away.

Why does he have to make it so hard? I never should've agreed to meet him after school. I only did it because I know my parents want me to hang out with friends. This way at least I don't have to lie and say I am when I'm not.

Kane is kind of my friend. I think. He's talked to me in class every single day since school started. Even when I don't say much in return, he still keeps talking and cracking jokes. It's easy to be around him. For once, I don't feel like I have to answer questions. Kane knows how to take a hint and change the subject.

Sharing his tray of fries and letting him tell me about all his past injuries is just going to give him false hope, though. I'm not sure if sitting next to Kane the first day of class was the best choice.

I spend the whole afternoon with Kane, watching his friends skate. I've never been to a skatepark before, or any place like it, and I wasn't lying when I told him it was really cool. You'll never catch *me* on those ramps or trying to slide down a rail, but watching the others is fun.

It's baffling to me that as often as he's injured himself, Kane continues to keep at it. Who in their right mind would inflict all that pain upon himself?

Kane offers to give me a lift home on his handlebars again, but the brief ride from school to the skatepark is enough excitement for one day. I call my mom instead, and she comes and picks me up at the front gate. Kane waves goodbye, then turns back to his friends.

"Who's your friend?" Mom asks. She's come straight from work and is wearing her dress slacks and a blouse. Her blazer is carefully hung on a hanger on the hook in the back of her SUV.

"Just a guy from school," I answer.

"Isn't he the same one from urgent care?"

"Yeah." I can't believe she remembers him from that long ago.

Mom grins and continues to pepper me with questions on the drive home. I give her brief one-word answers. I don't want to talk about Kane. I don't want to talk at all.

We finally pull into the garage. I grab my bag, dart into the house, and shut myself in my room. Before the door fully closes, Mom yells for me to be down for dinner in thirty minutes or else.

Glancing at the time on my phone, I throw myself on my bed. Out of habit, I pull up my Instagram account and cringe when the screen loads. An image of my ex-boyfriend pops up. His arm wrapped around some nameless blonde. My heart sinks because not even a year ago that had been me.

Seeing how quickly he's replaced me is salt rubbed in the wound. I may not have been in love with Bradley, but it still hurts the way things ended.

I should stop following him on social media. Rachel, too. Block them even. But I just can't bring myself to do it. Instead, I close the app and toss my phone face down on the bed beside me. Pulling my sketch pad from my backpack, I flip past the ocean waves I'd been working on and begin sketching a rose. Soon, my fingers are itching for a more interesting subject, so I flip to a new page and begin sketching Kane from memory.

"Summer! Dinner," Mom calls from downstairs.

Startled, I drop the pencil and look at what I've drawn so far. The outline of Kane's face, his lips pulled up in a smile, with the faint scar visible down the center. His eyes, crinkled with humor. I set it aside. It's a good start, but it needs a lot of refining. I'd noticed a few other scars on Kane's face when I'd been studying the one on his lip but didn't have the stories behind them yet. I have no doubt he'll be more than willing to share. He takes pride in what others see as failure.

I walk slowly down to the kitchen and find Mom setting a platter of grilled chicken on the table next to a bowl of creamed corn. The table is already set, and Mandy is in her seat.

"Could you grab the barbecue sauce from the fridge, hon?" Mom asks when she sees me enter the room.

"Sure." I pull open the fridge door and grab the barbecue sauce, as well as the hot sauce for Dad.

"No Dad again?" I ask, realizing the table is set for three.

"He called and said something came up with the case he's working on. He has to stay late."

"Oh, okay." I set the barbecue sauce on the table next to the chicken, then return the hot sauce to the fridge.

I take my seat at the table. Mom has my bag of pills out and is methodically checking the list, pulling out the necessary meds to go with dinner. About a week and a half ago I had to miss the first half of school one day for a checkup with my doctor, so my dosages have changed. Every time I think we've found the perfect cocktail of drugs, the doctors decide to change it, so consulting the list is a must.

Mom reaches over and sets the pills on my plate. Seeing the

tiny, innocent looking capsules is a daily reminder of the future I have to look forward to. Pills, pills, and more pills.

"Tell me about the boy from today." Mom cuts her chicken into bite size pieces, while Mandy fills her plate with corn. She's still going through her vegetarian phase. I hope Mom serves salad tomorrow.

"Summer has a new boyfriend?" Mandy asks. Her eyes are sparkling with delight. "When can I meet him?"

I gather the pills from my plate and swallow them one by one, chasing each with a gulp of water.

"Summer does *not* have a new boyfriend." I stare pointedly at my sister. "Summer hung out with her partner from class and a couple of his friends. That's it."

"Uh huh..." Mandy says, grinning with a mouth full of corn.

"Okay. No boyfriend," Mom concedes. "So, how's Rachel doing? I haven't seen her around in quite a while."

I cringe inwardly. It would be a lot easier if Mom knew Rachel and I weren't friends anymore, but I *really* don't want to get into it, so I lie.

"She's fine."

"You girls should have a sleepover next weekend," Mom suggests.

I nearly drop the piece of chicken I've just skewered from the platter. "Um...I'll see what she has going on." This is a lie. There is no way I'm going to ask Rachel to sleep over. Never in a million years.

"You were so isolated this summer," Mom continues. I take the corn bowl from the center of the table and drop a small scoop onto my plate. "I know you hate that you had to quit the volleyball team."

Here she goes...

"Just because you have this disease doesn't mean you have to give up everything you love though. Lots of people with lupus live very normal lives, you can too. We've got a pretty good handle on things already." Mom beams at me.

Right. A good handle on things. It's only been a month since my last visit to urgent care for a stupid fever. Any normal person would just take Tylenol and wait it out. Not me though. My stupid white blood cells are too busy fighting *themselves* to fight the actual intruder. Now every fever is potentially life threatening.

"I know, Mom," I mutter. I stab a piece of chicken and bring it to my lips. She's been telling me the same thing since my diagnosis. She can believe the words all she wants, but *I'm* the one who has to live with the disease. And I *don't* believe it. The life I know and love has, in fact, ended.

When we finish eating dinner, Mandy and I help Mom clean up, then I retreat to the sanctity of my bedroom again.

I return to the sketch of Kane and stare at it. His eyes don't seem quite right. I dig out last year's yearbook and squint at his photo. Frustrated, I put on the prescription lenses I got this summer and look again. He had on that same stupid, big, contagious grin he always has, and appears to be injury free, at least in the headshot. I study his eyes, looking back and forth between my sketch and his photo. Finally, I pick up my pencil and adjust the tilt, angling them upward just a smidge.

Satisfied with the result, I stare at the yearbook photo again. Kane really is cute, in an adorable kind of way. He's nothing like Bradley, who has a perfectly straight nose, perfectly spaced eyes, and no scars marring his acne-free skin.

Studying the photo closer, I realize Kane's nose is a little crooked—no doubt broken at least once. And of course there are the scars on his lip, chin, and forehead. Some might say these things take away from his looks, but I think they make him interesting. And that scares me. Because I do *not* want to get close to anyone right now...or ever.

I put the sketch away and push my glasses up on my nose. As if the rash and fevers weren't bad enough, my lupus has also started to kill my vision. I try to focus on homework for the rest of the evening, but when I begin yawning, I give up and change into my pajamas. Once my teeth are brushed and my face is washed, I lie in bed with the lights out, staring at the ceiling. I'm suddenly wide awake. Yet another side effect. Insomnia.

Giving up on sleep, I grab my phone and alternate between stalking my former friends on social media and playing a dumb game.

I must have eventually drifted off, because the next thing I know the sun is shining through my window. Mandy's footsteps thunder through the house. My bedroom door flies open, slamming into the door stop and bouncing back. I jerk upright with a start. Mandy is standing in my doorway dressed for school in shorts and a pink t-shirt. Her backpack is strapped to her back.

I blink at her, bleary eyed, trying to get my bearings.

"You're going to be late for school," Mandy says.

I blink again, then push my hair from my face. My phone is next to me on my bed, and when I grab it the screen is black. Clicking the power button, I realize the battery is dead. My alarm never had a chance to go off. Groaning, I throw my legs over the side of the bed. My joints are stiff, and I ache all over.

"How late am I?" I ask.

"Very." She races from my room, and I follow, still in my pajama shorts and t-shirt.

Mom is standing by the front door, frowning.

"I'm sorry, Summer. I thought you were already up."

I hold up my phone. "I guess my battery died."

Mom shakes her head. "You need to be better about charging that thing." She glances at the wall clock in the foyer and says, "I can't wait for you to get ready. You'll have to walk."

I nod. It's not that far of a walk. "Will you write me a note?"

"No time, I've got to get Mandy to school and get to the office. I'll call the school from the car and tell them you'll be late."

"Thanks, Mom."

"Don't forget sunscreen!" she calls after me as I retreat back up the stairs.

Each step a painful reminder of my disease. Mornings are the worst. After plugging my phone into my charger, I grab clothes for the day. I twist my hair into a bun on top of my head to keep dry and take a hot shower. It's no magical cure, but the hot water helps to ease some of the stiffness in my joints. By the time I'm dried off and dressed, I almost feel human again.

7

KANE

S pending yesterday afternoon with Summer at the skatepark was amazing. I think she had fun too, but I always have a hard time reading her. She's so guarded; it's like she's put up a wall between herself and everyone else. I wonder what's changed since last year, or maybe she's always been like this. Maybe I was just—as my dad would say—viewing her through rose colored glasses?

I walk into foods class, ready to interrogate her again. She's sitting with her head resting on the table, as I've seen her doing more days than not since the school year began.

"Don't you sleep at home, Sleeping Beauty?" I ask, pitching my voice soft and low so I don't startle her.

Summer doesn't answer. I look around to see if anyone else is watching, but they're all lost in their own lives.

"Hey, are you okay?" I ask a little louder. I sit down beside her and gently nudge her elbow with my own.

Summer starts, sitting bolt upright. She looks exhausted. I can see that she's tried to work her girly magic and hide the circles under her eyes, but it hasn't entirely worked. This is a girl who is severely sleep deprived.

Summer's eyes lock on mine for a moment, then she quickly stares at the table.

"Rough night?" I ask.

She gives me a sidelong look, then nods.

"Want to talk about it?"

She shakes her head.

"Okay." I reach in my bag and pull out my notebook and a pen, arranging them on the tabletop. I glance beside me and catch her staring at me.

"What?" I wipe at my mouth. "Do I have something on my face?"

The corners of her mouth quirk up, and she says, "No. You just always surprise me."

I raise an eyebrow. "Good surprise?"

"Yes."

"How so?" I'm curious. It seems like something I'm doing has impressed this beautiful girl, and I want to know what it is, so I can keep it up.

She shakes her head. "I said I didn't want to talk about it, and you let it go. Not many people do that. Not even my own parents."

I shrug. "I figure if you want to talk about it you will."

"Thank you."

"So, since I'm impressing you so much, how about that date?" I waggle my eyebrows at her and hope I'm not pressing my luck.

Her smile grows, and she turns her attention to the front of the room.

"That wasn't a no," I whisper as class begins.

She shakes her head, but her smile never fades.

Ms. Knope assigns us a worksheet to fill out with our partner, and I turn to Summer. She's digging through her bag for a pencil, rifling through textbooks, notebooks, and— "Is that a sketchbook?" I ask.

Her gaze darts to her bag, then back to me. "Maybe..."

"I didn't know you draw. Can I see?"

She shakes her head, her cheeks turning pink. I wonder what she's embarrassed about.

"Please?" I beg. I pout my lower lip and lean in close. "Pretty please with a cherry and whipped cream and sprinkles on top?"

"Wow, you look like the world's saddest puppy." She laughs.

"Better show me then to cheer me up." I bat my eyelashes for good measure.

"Fine." She reaches into her bag and pulls out her sketch pad. She flips it open and slides it across the table in front of me.

My gaze settles on the pencil sketch of the ocean on the page, and my jaw drops. I look between Summer and the sketch. All humor leaves my voice, and I say, "You seriously drew this?"

She shrugs. "Yeah."

"This is really good, Summer. Like, *really* good."

Her cheeks grow pinker and she tilts her head forward, her hair shielding her blush from my view.

I reach forward to flip the page, just as she reaches out and says, "No!"

But she's too slow. I've already seen what's on the next two pages. I ignore the rose on the second page, and leave the book open to the third. "Is that me?"

She shrugs and slumps low in her seat, giving up on trying to hide the sketch.

"Wow, you even got the break in my nose right."

She peeks at me from behind her hair. "How did you manage that anyway?"

I laugh. "Snowboarding. My dad took me to Colorado one year for winter break. Mom was *pissed* when I came back in bandages; Dad and I both got reamed out by her." I smile at the memory. "It was a lot of fun though."

"You do know that you're crazy, right? You just said that breaking your nose was fun."

I wave her off. "Well, the nose breaking part wasn't fun, but the rest of the trip was."

"A normal person would say, 'I broke my nose and it ruined my entire trip.'"

"I like to think I'm exceptional, not normal."

"Ms. Knope is coming," Summer says, just loud enough for me to hear. She quickly returns the sketchpad to her bag and pulls out a pencil. Together we fill out the worksheet. She's way better at finding the answers than me; another reason to be glad she's my partner.

"I still can't believe you drew those. If you want, I'll pose for you," I say once Ms. Knope has passed our table and returned to the front of the room.

Summer's cheeks blaze for a moment, before she shields herself behind a curtain of hair.

"I'm pretty sure if I tried to draw you, you'd probably just end up as a stick figure with spaghetti hair," I continue, as though I haven't just embarrassed her.

She pushes her hair behind one ear and smiles as she fills out the next answer on our worksheet. She designated herself as our scribe when she saw how terrible my handwriting is.

"We're all good at something different," she finally says.

"Oh, not me," I say with a laugh. "Ask anyone. I'm not good at anything."

Summer looks up and frowns. "That's not true."

I raise my eyebrows. "Name something I'm good at."

She blinks once, slowly, then in a voice that screams 'how do you not know this you moron,' she says, "Making me smile."

I'm speechless. The bell rings, and Summer picks up her backpack and slings it over her shoulder. She gives me one last parting smile, and then leaves the classroom.

The waves crash against the sandy beach and I can just make out Mark in the water. A tiny black dot on a blue and green board, waiting for the right moment. A large wave rolls in, and the tiny figure pops up on his board. Gradually, he grows larger as he rides the wave toward shore.

"You should have invited her with us today." Abigail sits beside me in the sand, a large floppy hat shielding her face from the sun. Leaning back on her forearms, she stares out at the Pacific.

"I would have. But she left me speechless."

"Right, that line about how you can make her smile."

Abigail and I sit in companionable silence for a few minutes. We watch the waves roll in and out, taking Mark with them.

"She's not wrong, you know," Abigail says, breaking the silence.

"Hmm?" I've already forgotten what we'd been talking about. I'm mesmerized by the calming rhythm of the ocean. Mark tried to teach me to surf, but I was a lost cause. I could ride the smallest of waves, sometimes, but the big ones were impossible for me. It was probably for the best though. I figured with my track record, I'd probably just be asking for a shark to swim up and take a bite out of me. No thank you.

"You may be a bit of a screw up with everything you do, but you never fail to make people laugh and smile," Abigail explains.

"So, what you're saying is, I have a future as a comedian?" I turn my attention from the waves and grin at her.

"Oh boy..." She eyes me critically and then rolls her eyes. "You're not *that* funny, Kane."

"You did just say I never fail to make people laugh."

"You're more like the guys from MTV's *Jackass*. Nobody wants another one of those guys around."

"Hmmph." I don't tell her that I want to follow in my dad's footsteps and be a stuntman. I've never told anyone that. Not even my dad. I know my friends and family love and support me, but I'm also painfully aware that I'm prone to injury. Pun intended. I don't want to give them the opportunity to crush my dreams before I can even give it a shot.

"So, what's your next move?" she asks.

"What do you mean?"

"I mean, *what's your next move?*" She looks at me like I'm an idiot. Which I probably am. "You've asked her out twice, and she's turned you down twice. Now what?"

"I'd like to point out that she didn't actually say *no* the second time. She didn't really say anything at all."

"In girl speak, that means no."

I shoot her a glare. "I don't know if your opinion counts in this matter."

Abigail scoffs. "Why? Because I like girls?"

I don't say anything, instead I focus on scooping a handful of sand and let it trickle through my fingers.

"If anything, that should make me even *more* of an expert in this matter. I *am* a girl, and I've been *rejected* by girls."

I turn my attention back to her. "Since when have *you* ever been rejected?" This is the first I've heard of it. Abigail is gorgeous. She has shoulder-length natural red hair—the kind she claims could never come from a bottle. Her skin is ivory, and she has a badass fashion sense—all her words, not mine. The idea of anyone, gay or straight, saying no to Abigail blows my mind.

She rolls her eyes. "Everyone gets turned down at some point, Kane."

"How did I not know this?"

"Because not everyone obsesses over a person like you do."

"Hey," I object. "I'm not obsessed."

She raises her eyebrows, daring me to fight her on this.

"Okay, maybe a little. But this is the real deal." She shoots me another look, and I add, "I'm not just obsessed with how she looks. I like talking to her."

"Well, that's something."

I grin. This is probably as close to Abigail's approval as I'll get.

"How much longer do you think he'll be out there?" She shields her eyes from the afternoon glare reflecting off the water and scans the surf for Mark. "He knows I'll get scorched by the sun if I'm out here too long."

"Hey, you're the one who insists on coming out here with us."

"If I didn't, who would help you warm the bench."

"A cheesy sports metaphor? Really?" I playfully shove her, and she laughs.

"You never did answer me," she says.

"Huh?"

"What's your next move with Summer."

I shrug. "Wait for my next opportunity to ask her out, I guess. In the meantime, I'm going to keep trying to get to know her and hang out with her."

"Try not to scare her off. She seems nice."

I shove her lightly again and try to hide my smile.

8

SUMMER

Repetition is my life these days. Wake up achy and stiff, go to school, come home and have dinner with my family, go to my room and do homework, then try—and usually fail—to sleep.

Tonight is no different, except it's a rare night with Dad home in time for dinner. I take my seat at the table with my parents and Mandy, going through the same motions as every other night. Mom is dishing food onto her plate. Dad is trying to hide his phone in his lap, working even at the dinner table.

I swallow my pills and fill my own plate, pushing my food around and picking at it. I force down a bit so my pills don't sit in an empty stomach. I don't have much of an appetite tonight, but I make an effort, to keep my parents off my back. I don't have to try too hard because Dad's attention has shifted from his screen to Mandy, his expression confused.

"Is that all you're eating?" he asks.

"I'm a vegetarian now," she tells him. "It's wrong to eat cute little animals."

"Huh." Dad drops it and returns to his own dinner.

"What did Rachel say?" Mom asks.

"Hmm?"

"Rachel? You were going to ask her about having a slumber party this weekend."

I roll my eyes. "Mom, nobody calls it a slumber party."

Mom shoots me a glare. "Cut the sass. You know what I mean, Summer."

I shrug. "She can't make it."

"Oh, that's too bad." Mom looks and sounds seriously disappointed. "Maybe some other time."

"Hmm," I make a noncommittal noise; not a confirmation or a denial.

"You've been spending too much time locked up in your room," Dad says. He's rarely home, so I don't know how he knows this.

I glance at him and say, "I'm a teenager. Isn't that what we do? Lock ourselves in our rooms and only come out for meals?"

Mandy giggles, and Dad frowns. He still looks young, though his dark hair is going silver at the temples, his blue eyes are still bright. I get my eyes from him; my blonde hair comes from my mom. But when Dad frowns, his true age shows.

"Maybe that's true for other teenagers, but not my daughter." The look he gives me is severe, and I avert my eyes. He sighs and goes on. "You can't lock yourself up for the rest of your life. You need to get back to the way things were."

I stab at the asparagus on my plate a little too fiercely. The way things were? Yeah right. In what universe is *that* possible?

"Listen sweetie," Mom interjects. "Dad and I were talking. We'd like you to see someone, to talk about how you're feeling."

"I don't need a shrink, Mom!" Like I'm not a big enough freak already, let's add therapy? No way.

"Summer, we realize there is an adjustment period, but we're worried about you." Dad's voice is firm. I have a feeling they've rehearsed this speech.

"Honey, if you could show us that things are getting back to normal we could reconsider the therapy idea." Mom's voice is much softer than Dad's. If this was good cop/bad cop, Mom would definitely be good cop.

"I see people at school all day long. And I hung out with my foods class partner, like, four days ago."

"You've been back to school for weeks, and you've spent time with friends once. We'd like you to have someone over, get back to how things used to be."

"So, what? If I have a *slumber party* I don't have to talk about my feelings?" I demand, alternating my glare between my parents.

They exchange a look, then Mom says, "It would be a start."

"Fine. I'll get someone to sleep over this weekend." I stare at my nearly full plate. "May I please be excused? I'm not very hungry."

Mom and Dad exchange another look, sharing a silent conversation, before Dad says, "Sure."

After clearing my place at the table, I hurry to my room and throw the door shut. I collapse onto my bed. Crap, crap, crap. Not only do I need to find someone to sleep over this weekend, I need to ensure I have enough energy for the sleepover.

Tomorrow is Tuesday, so I have a few days to figure this out. I mentally scroll through the list of girls I know and scratch each of them off in turn. They were all a part of my old life. The life where I was healthy and a part of the team. What other girls did I know?

Then it hits me. I met Kane's friends at the skatepark and one of them was a girl. What was her name...Abigail? It would be *so* awkward to ask her to hang out. We probably have nothing in common. But my alternative is therapy, and there is *no way* I'm going through with that. I have enough doctors in my life, I don't need one for my head too.

I've made up my mind. By Thursday, I'll work up the nerve to ask Abigail if she's available to hang out.

I slip on my glasses and pull out my Chemistry textbook. It doesn't take long before I give up on reading the assigned pages.

My mind won't focus. Instead, I pull out my sketchpad and fine-tune my drawing of Kane. I add a skateboard to the background, then a snowboard. My eyes grow tired, and I fall asleep fully clothed on top of my blankets.

The alarm blaring on my phone jolts me awake. I'm surprised to find I've slept solidly through the night. It's been a while since that's happened. I smile to myself; I feel well rested and optimistic. Today will be a good day. At lunch, I'll ask Abigail to sleep over.

I breeze through my morning classes, but as lunch draws near, butterflies begin to take flight in my stomach. Am I really going to ask a girl I've met *once* to sleep over at my house? What if she says no? Or, god, what if she says *yes*? I remind myself that I don't have to ask her right away. I can wait. But if the opportunity presents itself, I'm going to take it.

The bell rings, and the moment of truth is on the horizon. I make a detour on my way to the cafeteria to take my pills. I discovered weeks ago that it's less conspicuous to get my meds at the beginning of lunch period rather than the end. I leave Ms. Hall's office, and before I can get halfway down the hall, I'm stopped by Mr. Kaiser.

"Summer." He's grinning, as he flags me down. "I was hoping I'd run into you soon."

"What's up, Mr. K?" I'm filled with dread. I know what he's going to say.

"The sign-up sheet for stage crew has been up for a little while. I saw Rachel on the list, but I didn't see your name."

I shift my weight from foot to foot. "Yeah, I'm...not really doing any extracurriculars this year. Really focusing on my classes."

"That's too bad. You were the best person I had for makeup and wardrobe. I know you were thinking of trying to get into stage makeup after high school. This would look good on your applications. Are you sure you won't reconsider?"

"I really can't. I'm sorry." I take a couple steps back from him.

"I have to get to lunch. Bye." I turn and hurry down the hall toward the cafeteria.

"At least consider coming back for the spring musical," he calls after me.

I hear his words, but I can't do that. I can't help with the plays. It would be unfair to everyone if I got really sick again when they were counting on me. Not to mention how painful it would be to spend that much time around Rachel.

Feeling defeated and emotionally drained, I rush through the lunch line. I carry my tray to my secluded table in the courtyard and take in my surroundings. The brick walls of the school are plastered with posters for homecoming. I overhear a group of younger girls at a table nearby giggling about boys and the dance. My gaze skims over faces, some familiar, some not, and eventually settles on Kane across the courtyard.

I feel a stab of jealousy as I watch him and his friends. Kane is talking animatedly, waving his arms around. Abigail rolls her eyes, and Mark shakes his head, a small smile on his lips. I shift my gaze to my lunch tray, avoiding the people around me.

I'd always heard of feeling alone while surrounded by people, but I never understood it. I do now.

9

KANE

I've given Summer her space outside of class. Every day, she eats alone, tucked away in her own corner of the courtyard in the shade of the building. Every day, I make a point to try and catch her eye and wave. But today something is different. I've seen her glancing over at my table, but she's quick to look away. For a girl who always seems so lonely, today she seems particularly sad.

"Hey guys, I've gotta go," I interrupt Abigail. I'm not sure what she's talking about. I've been so distracted watching Summer for the past few minutes that I wasn't paying much attention to my friends. I think I caught something about tattoos and sea turtles, but I really can't say.

"Go talk to your woman," Abigail says on a sigh.

I shoot her a grin, then gather up my backpack and lunch.

I cross the courtyard and set my bag down on the bench across from Summer. "Hi."

"Oh, hey, Kane." She looks at me for a moment, then returns her focus to her lunch.

"So, what's new?"

She shrugs and continues to stare at her lunch tray, pushing her food around without eating it. This is harder than I thought it would be.

"Don't feel much like talking?"

Another shrug.

"Well, I've got some good news," I say brightly. "I'm having my cast taken off next week."

Her gaze flickers to my cast, which is even more beat up now than it was when she signed it a few weeks ago. "So you'll get your board back?" she asks softly.

Score. She's speaking.

"That's the plan. Unless the doctor says something to make my mom change her mind." I scrunch up my face at the thought, and a smile tugs at the corners of her lips.

"You're not going to try to do that...grind thing again, are you?" she asks.

"Well, not immediately. I mean, if I *happen* to fall again and break something so soon, Mom might *never* give my board back."

She laughs. "You really are crazy."

"I prefer adorable." I wink, wondering if she remembers that I've already used this line on her. She shakes her head, but her smile remains.

I continue to talk with her for the rest of the lunch period, and she seems happier now than she was before I showed up. Our conversation ends all too soon when the end of period bell rings. "Can I walk you to class?" I ask.

She opens her mouth, but before she can say anything, I quickly add, "I mean, we *are* going to the same place, right?"

She pushes her hair behind her ears, then says, "Okay. Sure."

We stand, and I grab her lunch tray. I'm trying to win brownie points in the chivalry department. The small smile that tugs at the corners of her lips at the gesture is becoming familiar. My goal is to make that smile more permanent.

We stop at Summer's locker, then walk to foods class. It's not until we're settled in our seats that I notice a dark-haired girl watching us. I give her a little wave and she quickly turns around, averting her gaze to the front of the room. Turning back to Summer, I see her smile has faded, replaced by a scowl. I wonder what's up with that.

"Do you have any brothers or sisters?"

"Huh?" she asks. The scowl fades from her lips and her brow is doing the cute scrunched up thing it does when she's caught by surprise.

"Brothers or sisters?" I repeat. "I'm an only child. What about you?"

"Oh, um, I have a little sister."

"Is that a good thing or a bad thing?"

The tiny sliver of a smile returns. "Usually a good thing."

"Tell me about her."

"What's to tell? She's eleven."

"What's her name?" She's saying more than she usually says. Maybe talking about something other than her is the right way to go.

"Mandy."

"And you and Mandy get along?"

"Most of the time. She's been extra nice ever since..." She bites her lip. There she goes with the secrets again.

"I always wanted a brother. My mom says that one of me is more than enough."

Summer laughs. "I'm not surprised."

It feels good to hear her laugh, especially because of something I said.

"My sister has recently decided that she's a vegetarian," she says. "Family dinners have become quite interesting."

I laugh. "Are your parents making tofu every night now?"

"No, thank god." She shakes her head, rolling her eyes. "They're just making extra veggies. The expression on her face while she eats is kind of hilarious. Especially the green beans. She *hates* green beans."

"Do you hate the green beans too?" I prop my elbow on the desk, resting my head in my hand, and study her. Her face lights up when she talks about her sister, it's a new side of Summer I haven't seen before, and I like it.

"I could live a happy life without ever tasting another green bean." She smiles at me, and though it's not quite a full smile, she lights the room up just the same.

"I'm also a part of the green bean hating club," I say. "We should make t-shirts."

"I'd wear mine proudly."

"So, you hate green beans. But what do you love? What's your favorite snack?"

"Gummy bears."

"Really?"

She nods.

"Just gummy bears? Or are gummy worms acceptable? What about Sour Patch Kids?"

She shakes her head. "I'll eat those, but gummy bears are the best. I like to eat the heads first."

"Vicious. You're not as sweet as you look, huh?"

Pink creeps into her cheeks and she tips her head forward, her hair blocking her face from my view.

She's saved from any further commentary from me when the bell rings, and Ms. Knope calls the class to order. I mentally file away all the little details I've just learned for later.

10

SUMMER

I can't believe I wussed out on asking Abigail to sleep over yesterday. The day had started so promising. But all it took was that brief conversation with Mr. Kaiser to ruin everything. I thought I was coping pretty well with everything I've had to give up, but his encouraging me to come back to stage crew triggered something.

Today will be different. Nothing will stop me. I will sit with Kane at lunch, and *today* I will ask Abigail to sleep over.

Stepping out of the cafeteria, I scan the courtyard for Kane and his friends. *I can do this.* He's made it no secret he's interested in me, so there's no reason he wouldn't want me to sit with him.

When I spot him, he's at his usual table, sitting across from Mark.

I take a deep breath and pull my shoulders back. With my chin held high, I march right up to their table. I pause a few feet from Kane, a smile on my face, and say, "Can I join you?"

Kane and Mark both freeze, mouths open in surprise. My smile falters and my fingers curl around the edges of my lunch tray. The plastic ridges dig into my skin. My heart pounds in my chest.

This was stupid. You don't just walk up to someone else's lunch table and make yourself at home. I should take my lunch and run away before I make an even bigger fool of myself.

But then the shock disappears from Kane's face, replaced by a grin. "Of course you can."

I glance at Mark. He smirks and gives me a nod. I take that as an invitation to stay, and my grip on the tray relaxes. I release an uneasy breath, and my heart rate slows.

"So, Summer, what's up?" Mark asks.

I shrug. "Not much. You?"

Mark has a ridiculous grin on his face, and he keeps looking at Kane. I feel like the butt of a joke.

"Ow!" Mark flinches, jerking back in his seat. He glares at Kane. I've clearly missed something.

"What brings you to our table today?" Kane asks, pulling my attention away from Mark.

"I just thought it might be nice to sit with people again." I stare down at my tray. This isn't really true. I'd be a lot more comfortable sitting alone. But short of showing up at the skatepark, this is the only time I know for sure I'll see Abigail.

"Awesome. You're always welcome at this table," Kane says. He's grinning that big goofy grin of his, and I can't help but smile back.

"Thanks." I glance around. "Where's the third member of your crew?"

Kane shrugs, and his eyes light up in amusement. "Who cares?"

"Rude."

I spin around in time to see Abigail smack Kane in the back of the head with her palm. She walks around the table and sits beside Mark. Kane laughs and rubs the back of his head.

"You better watch it, mister," Abigail says. She sets down her lunch tray and shakes her fork at him. The words are harsh, but her tone is light, and I can see a twinkle in her eyes. I have a feeling this is how they always are together.

Abigail turns her attention to me. "Are you sure you want to sit with us misfits?"

"Watching you guys is cheaper than going to the movies and more entertaining."

Abigail beams. She looks between Kane and Mark, and says, "I like her. She can stay."

I try not to let my face betray how her words make me feel, but the corners of my lips fight to tug upward. They've accepted me. I knew Kane would, he already has, but I wasn't so sure about his friends. Now it's time to prime them before I go in for the kill.

"Do you guys have big plans for the weekend?" I ask, pushing a soggy French toast stick around in the syrup on my tray. I wonder if it's worth eating. I should have gotten something from the salad bar instead.

"Nothing concrete," Kane says, pulling a brown paper bag from his backpack and producing a PB&J sandwich. He takes a bite, and with his mouth full says, "Maybe the beach?"

"Gross, Kane," Abigail chastises. He flashes her a huge grin, grape jelly sticking to the corner of his mouth.

"Oh, definitely the beach," Mark says, ignoring their tangent. He shoves an entire French toast stick in his mouth, clearly not bothered by the texture.

"What do you guys do at the beach?" I ask, before resigning myself to a bite of my unappetizing lunch.

Mark swallows. "Surf."

"People watch," says Abigail.

"Just hang out," Kane says.

"Wait." I look at Kane in surprise. "You don't surf?"

Mark laughs. "He's pitiful. You've seen what happens when he's on solid ground."

"Thanks a lot, *friend*."

"We only speak the truth." Abigail rolls her eyes and takes a bite of her lunch.

"*We* know it's true, but *she* didn't. You could've at least let me pretend for a while that I'm cooler than I actually am." He sighs in defeat.

"Well, technically you already told me you aren't good at anything, so you'd already set the bar pretty low."

His eyes twinkle and he laughs. "I did say that." He pauses a moment, lost in thought. "I suppose I'll forgive my so-called friends."

"Gee, thanks," Abigail says, her voice laced with sarcasm.

Kane ignores her remark, turning in his seat so he's looking directly at me. "Wanna join us at the beach on Saturday?"

"Oh, um..."

"Don't feel obligated," Mark says. "He can be pushy."

"But you *are* welcome," Abigail adds with a friendly smile.

"Well, okay. Sure."

Kane pumps his fist beside me. He's grinning ear to ear.

I'm in. Now I just have to figure out how to ask Abigail to sleep over. No time like the present. "So, um, Abigail."

She looks up from her lunch and watches me curiously. "Yeah?"

I force a laugh and rush to say, "So, I sort of had to quit the volleyball team, and most of my friends were from the team, but now that *I'm* not on the team we don't really hang out anymore."

Abigail furrows her brow at me and waits.

I'm rambling. And talking way too fast. Crap.

I force myself to slow down and continue. "Anyway, I sort of promised my parents that I've made new friends. And I would have someone sleep over this weekend. And that was basically a lie, because the only people I've talked to outside of class are you three."

And now I sound like a complete loser.

There's a moment of silence. I ignore the boys and force my gaze to stay on Abigail. It takes her a moment as she digests everything I've just said.

"Are you asking me to sleep over this weekend?" Abigail finally asks.

"Yes?"

Abigail grins. She glances at Kane, then says, "Sure!"

"Really?" I let out my second breath of relief of the day. I can't believe how easy this was. Why was I freaking out? "You're a lifesaver."

Abigail waves me off. "No big deal. This will be fun. I hang out with these two doofuses all the time. It'll be nice to hang out with a girl for a change."

Kane groans beside me and I ignore him.

"Great!"

Then a new panic hits me. Somehow, I have to keep my parents and sister from mentioning anything about my lupus. My parents will keep quiet, I'm sure, but Mandy? She's a wild card.

11

KANE

I ditch my bike at the racks and storm past Dennis, who is sitting on the wall outside the skatepark.

"How did *you* end up with *my* date?" I demand, running up one of the smaller ramps and confronting Abigail. This is the first time I've had a chance to speak with her since lunch. I'm still in disbelief over the whole sleepover thing.

Abigail laughs as she sails past me and up the other side of the ramp. She's getting way too much enjoyment out of this.

I hop down and glare at her. Knowing she'll pause soon, I wait.

Sure enough, she glides to a stop in front of me and steps off her board. "Come on Kane, it's just a sleepover." She grins mischievously.

"It better be." I stoop low, snag her board, and take off running before she can stop me.

"Hey!"

I grin, drop the board on the cement, and step on. I push off and skirt around the large ramps. Throwing a glance over my shoulder at Abigail, I see she's still standing where I'd abandoned her. Hands on her hips, she shoots daggers at me. At least she isn't laughing anymore. I let out my own laugh, loud and maniacal.

"Your mom is going to kill you!" she yells.

"Only if she finds out!" I holler back.

I circle around Abigail twice before jumping off and letting the board roll past us.

"Tell me everything that happens at this sleepover," I demand.

Abigail walks away to retrieve her board and glares at me. "No way you perv. Sleepovers are a sacred thing."

"Seriously, Abz? Have all these years of friendship meant nothing?"

She just stares at me, the glare still on her face.

"I'd do it for you, you know."

"Oh, really?" She raises her eyebrows at me. "You're going to have a sleepover with a girl I'm crushing on?"

A sound almost like a growl escapes my mouth. She's killing me. "You know what I mean."

Abigail laughs. "Yeah, I do. And if I tell you anything, it'll be a very general picture of the night. No specifics."

"I'll take what I can get." I take a seat on one of the benches and pull out my phone, contenting myself with a dumb app game while my friends have the real fun. This cast can't come off soon enough. Maybe Mom will see reason and give my board back early. Yeah, right.

The front door opens and Mom walks in, arms full of groceries. It's a typical Saturday morning.

"Care to give your mother a hand, Kane?" she calls.

I hop up from my seat at the kitchen table and grab one of the bags from her arms.

"What are your plans today?" she asks, setting her bag on the kitchen counter. I snoop through the bag I've just set down as mom unloads hers.

"Just hanging at the beach with my friends," I tell her, pulling out a bag of Chex Mix.

"Say hi to Mark and Abigail for me." Mom snatches the bag from my hand before I can open it. "And don't forget to video chat your dad at four."

"Will do."

Mom gives me *The Look*.

"I'll remember, Mom."

I may have lost track of time a couple times and missed my scheduled calls with Dad, but it's been at *least* a month since the last time. I'm on a roll.

"What are the odds of me getting my board back?" I pull the most innocent face I can muster. "Just for today."

"Kane..." There's a warning tone in her voice.

"No ramps or rails," I promise. "Just the boardwalk at the beach. Totally safe."

Her look doesn't falter.

"And listen, even if I *were* to fall, I'll be surrounded by soft sand to cushion the blow."

"Who else is going with you?"

I can see the start of a smile at the corner of her lips. I might be in if I play my cards right.

"Just...a girl..." I try to be casual and busy myself with the glass sugar jar on the counter, lining it up perfectly with the jar of flour.

Out of the corner of my eye, I see Mom raise her eyebrows.

I give up on playing cool. I turn to face Mom and plead, "Her name is Summer, and she's the prettiest girl I've ever seen—after you of course." I flash her a sweet smile. "And I promised to teach her to ride a skateboard."

Okay, that's a stretch. But those words *had* come out of my mouth at one point so it wasn't *really* a lie.

She studies me for a moment, eyes narrowed. "*Just today*," Mom caves.

"Yes!" I pump my fist in the air.

"Do *not* make me regret this." She retreats to her office and returns with my skateboard.

I hug the board to my chest and then kiss the surface.

Mom makes a disgusted face, and says, "You're a little too much like your father sometimes..."

I take that as a compliment and grin at my board. "I've missed you baby," I whisper.

Shaking her head, she returns to unloading the grocery bags, and I leave the house.

Mark and I are waiting impatiently at his car—well, I'm impatient; Mark is chill as always—when Abigail finally exits her house. She's dressed casually for the beach, complete with her oversized hat and sunglasses.

"Hurry up!" I yell across the yard. We're meeting Summer at the boardwalk and we're already late.

Even from this distance, I can see her eyes roll. If I thought she couldn't move slower, I was wrong, because she does.

Groaning, I open the back door and toss my board on the seat.

"Kane has his board back?" Abigail approaches the car and raises her eyebrows at me.

"How the hell did you convince her to give you the board back anyway?" Mark asks, shaking his head in disbelief as he slides in behind the wheel. He has his wetsuit on, and his surfboard strapped to the roof of the car.

I shrug, climbing in next to my board. Abigail is in the front passenger side. "I can be very convincing."

"You've got your mom wrapped around your little finger. Why can't you give the poor woman a break and let her parent you properly?" Abigail comments.

"She's doing a wonderful job raising me."

"I'm surprised child protective services haven't been called out. Doesn't your dad get concerned by all your accidents?" Abigail eyes me in the rearview mirror.

I grin at her reflection from the backseat. "Stuntman, remember?"

"Pretty sure he told me that *you've* broken more bones in your *life* than he has in his *career*," Mark says. I can see his smirk in the mirror.

"You two are the *worst* best friends ever."

"Aww, it's only because we care about you." Abigail's eyes gleam with mirth.

We finally arrive at the beach, and Mark finds a parking spot. We all pile out and Mark sets off to hit the waves, while Abigail and I hit the boardwalk with our skateboards.

"Where is she meeting us?" Abigail asks.

My gaze darts up and down the boardwalk, and I point. "There."

Summer is standing on the boardwalk, looking uncomfortable, under the awning outside Sandy's Smoothie Shack.

"She looks thrilled to be here," Abigail notes dryly.

"She's probably just nervous. She's alone and has been waiting for who knows how long." I elbow her in the ribs.

We'd agreed to meet at eleven and it was now eleven fifteen thanks to Abigail's need to apply fifteen coats of eyeliner. Okay, I'm making that up. I don't actually know anything about makeup, but I do know that Abigail *does* wear a lot of goop on her eyes. And Mark and I *did* waste precious time waiting for her to finally meet us at the car.

I push off hard on my board, eager to meet up with Summer. As I approach the Smoothie Shack, I come to a stumbling stop. Summer looks unimpressed with, and a little surprised by, my clumsy approach. I beam at her. Abigail comes to a much more graceful stop moments later.

"Hey, girlfriend," Abigail says cheerfully, waving a hand in greeting. She pulls off her red, cat eye sunglasses and smiles at Summer.

Summer looks between the two of us. She seems unsure what to make of us.

"Hey," I say, tipping my own turquoise sunglasses down my nose to get a better look at her. She's wearing jean shorts and a blue tee, a pair of black sunglasses sit on the rim of the floppy straw hat on her head. There's a glittery cactus slung over her shoulder—I think it's a purse.

"Hey," Summer echoes. She looks around and frowns. "Where's Mark?"

I can't help it; I'm a little annoyed that she's asking where Mark is. *I'm* the one who wanted her to come today.

I casually wave off her question. "He's already hitting the waves."

Abigail rolls her eyes. "He's always so afraid of missing the *perfect wave*. He makes a beeline for the water as soon as the car is in park."

"Oh. Okay. So, what's the game plan?"

I pick up my skateboard, then gesture at the board with my cast hand, as if showing off a prize on a game show. "Look what I have."

"I thought you weren't getting it back until your wrist healed."

"Let's just say I convinced my mom to let me out on parole. I only get her back for the day, so we have to make the most of our time."

"Wait...we?" Summer looks between me and the board.

"Oh, yeah. I promised to teach you how to skate."

"I distinctly remember telling you no." She crosses her arms over her chest and looks wary.

"'*No*' isn't in Kane's vernacular. He doesn't know what it means, so he chooses not to hear it."

I glare at Abigail and shake my head. "Not helping." I do know what no means. I respect boundaries on important things. But this? Getting her on a board? I want to make this happen at *least* once.

"Sorry. I'll just leave you to it then." She puts her sunglasses on and skates away. I'm left alone with Summer.

"You're seriously going to make me get on that thing?"

I nod then set the board down on the smooth pavement.

"As long as you can keep your balance, you'll be fine. Watch." I step onto the board with one foot and use the other to push off slowly. I coast a few feet down the boardwalk before jumping off. I grin at her. "Your turn."

"If I break something, you're dead."

I ignore her threat and watch as she approaches me, looking warily at the board between us. Her gaze flicks up to me, her blue eyes large and questioning. "So, I just step on?"

I nod and push my sunglasses up into my hair. "Watch your balance, you don't want it to slide out from under you."

Summer, still looking worried, hesitantly steps on. Her gaze is glued to the board, which immediately begins to slip out from beneath her gray sneakers. I quickly step forward and reach out to steady her, catching her waist between my hands. She grabs my arms, her nails biting into my skin, and stumbles toward me.

Summer's eyes are wide as her gaze trails from the ground and up to meet mine. She's only a few inches away, her chin tipped up to look at me. Her familiar coconut scent is stronger than it's ever been, and she's so close I can see that her eyes aren't just blue; they're sapphire and azure, cornflower and midnight. They're mesmerizing. Her lips are slightly parted, still surprised by her misadventure on the skateboard. It takes all the self-control I possess not to lean forward and steal a kiss.

We're frozen for a moment, my hands at her waist, and hers tightly grasping my arms. I know there are people strolling past us on the boardwalk, but I don't see them, don't hear them. There's just Summer and me.

Then she drops her hands and steps back, her gaze focused on the boardwalk beneath our feet. Reluctantly, I release her waist, and wonder if I've blown my chance, if I should have just kissed her.

"Your board is getting away," she says, her voice just above a whisper.

Cursing, I chase after the board, grabbing it just before it veers off the side of the boardwalk and into the sand.

I turn back to Summer and grin. "Maybe we should call it quits." She looks relieved. "But just for the day. I'm not giving up on you yet."

12

SUMMER

Kane casually slips his right arm around my shoulder, the plaster of the cast resting on the neckline of my t-shirt. I stiffen at his touch then force my muscles to relax. It's just an arm. It isn't like he's trying to cop a feel or something. And as much as I hate to admit it, I *like* how this feels.

My terrifying moment on the skateboard replays in my mind. I've never felt so unsteady in my life. When Kane caught me, his hands on my waist, my heart raced. And not entirely from the near fall. I can still feel the warmth of his fingers.

I'd felt a spark when our eyes met; It scares me. I don't want anyone getting close to me. Maybe it was a mistake coming out with Kane and his friends. Even if it does get my parents off my back, I'm not sure I'm equipped to handle whatever *this* is.

Pushing the negative thoughts away, I cast my gaze around the beach and try and enjoy the moment. My heart sinks when it falls on a group of our classmates playing volleyball. I should be out there. Stupid disease. Just to come to the beach today I had to slather my skin in prescription strength sunscreen and promise my mom I'd reapply every couple hours.

"Wanna see if we can join the game?"

Kane's question startles me. I hadn't realized my longing was that obvious.

"No, let's keep going." I pick up the pace, as we stroll down the boardwalk.

"Should we stop for ice cream?" Kane gestures to a truck with a blue and white striped awning parked nearby.

"Sure." Maybe ice cream will distract me. It couldn't hurt.

We wait for two other customers to order and receive their ice cream, then step forward.

"Double scoop, cookie dough, waffle cone," Kane says to the teen boy in the window. He turns to me. "Summer?"

"Chocolate sugar cone, please. Single scoop."

"You sure you don't want a double?" Kane asks.

"I'm good." I reach for my purse to pay for my cone, but Kane beats me to it. A minute later, a girl steps out from the back of the truck, leans around the boy who took our order, and hands us our cones.

"Should we find somewhere shady to eat these?" Kane asks.

I nod, grateful for the suggestion. The more time out of the sun the better.

It's September, so even though the beach is crowded, it isn't as bad as it would have been a few weeks ago. There's the group at the volleyball nets, and the tables on the east side of the boardwalk are all occupied by couples, families, and groups of friends. From the boardwalk to the water, people sprawl about on beach towels, soaking up the rays. Blankets and coolers litter the sand.

"How about there?" I point toward a patch of sand at one end of the beach that falls in the shadow of the rocky cliff. It's so far down the beach most people don't bother.

"Good eyes," Kane says, and we begin walking down the board-walk toward the shady spot.

Armed with his ice cream cone and skateboard, Kane no longer has his arm around my shoulders. I feel both relief and a pang of remorse. I don't *want* to want his arm around me, but I do. Kane is a complication in my already complicated life, but I can't deny how nice and comforting it feels.

We reach the spot and stake our claim. Kane flops down first, sending up a spray of sand. I sit more carefully, preferring not to eat the beach with my dessert.

"So." Kane takes a bite out of his ice cream. He looks at me, vanilla on the tip of his nose, and says, "Top five favorite movies. Go."

"Uh…" Kane has a talent for catching me off guard. It seems like he just says the first thing that pops into his head. "You go first."

"Nope. I asked you."

I groan. "Okay. Top five movies of all time." I'm stalling, flipping through my favorite movies in my head and trying to narrow them down. "Uh… *Say Anything, The Princess Bride, Mean Girls, Can't Buy Me Love*, and *The Breakfast Club*."

Kane blinks at me, his face scrunched up. "I've heard of at least one of those."

I laugh. "I know, I have weird taste in movies. I like a lot of the 80's teen classics. I grew up watching them with my mom."

"Of those five, which is your absolute favorite?"

I answer with no hesitation. "*Say Anything*."

"Why?"

I shrug. Scooping up a pile of sand with my free hand, I let it trickle through my fingers. "I don't know. It's about two people from different worlds who shouldn't be together. When her world comes crashing down, he's there for her anyway, he doesn't judge her. They accept one another exactly as they are. Plus, Lloyd is *so* romantic."

"Got it. Romance is the key to your heart."

I roll my eyes and try to hide my smile. "Every girl wants romance."

Kane asks me more questions, my top five bands or artists, top five TV shows, and so on. I wonder if he's found an interrogation list on the Internet, or if he's naturally destined to work for some clickbait website someday.

This goes on for hours but feels like minutes. Kane is easy to be around, and I'm actually enjoying myself. For the first time in months I'm not pretending.

His phone buzzes, and he pauses in his questioning. His eyes skim the screen, and his face falls. "Crap. Sorry, I have to video chat my dad."

"Oh," I say. "I don't mind waiting."

"Thanks." He taps his screen, opening his video chat app. I expect him to wander off somewhere for privacy, but he remains seated beside me. I try not to be nosy, but I can't stop myself from glancing at his screen.

"Hey, Kid!" An upbeat male voice floats out of the phone's speaker.

"Hey, Dad. How's it hanging?"

"Very carefully."

Kane and his father laugh, and I'm left wondering what the big joke is.

"Where are you?" his dad asks.

"The beach."

"With Mark and Abigail?"

"They're around here somewhere." His face brightens, and he casts a glance at me. "Hey, say hi to my new friend, Summer." Kane angles his phone so that I'm in the frame.

"Hi, Mr. Dwyer." I have a better view of the screen now, and I can see the resemblance between Kane and his father. They share the same shade of medium-brown hair and the same infectious grin. You can't look at either one of them without wanting to smile yourself.

"It's nice to meet you, Summer. Call me Crash, everyone else does."

I catch Kane rolling his eyes beside me, and I pause upon hearing the nickname.

"Nice to meet you too."

Kane and his father chat for a little while longer, and I take the opportunity to reapply my sunscreen. I used to love the coconut scent, but by this point, I'm sick of it. It's become another reminder of my lupus. I should have reapplied a couple hours ago, but we've been in the shade, so I figure I'll be all right.

As I rub the lotion into my skin, I can't help but listen to Kane's conversation. From what I can gather, his dad works in Hollywood as a stuntman. I'm beginning to understand Kane a little better now. Understand where his impulsive—and somewhat crazy—personality comes from.

When Kane disconnects from the video chat with his dad, he grins at me.

"So that's your dad, huh?" I say.

"Yep. Having divorced parents is *awesome.*" He casts his eyes to the sky, his words oozing sarcasm. "I live with my mom, but Dad and I video chat at least once a week, and I go visit him in Hollywood as much as I can."

"That sucks."

He shrugs. "Yeah. Wanna know the worst part?"

I nod.

"I'm pretty sure they still love each other."

I keep quiet, wondering if Kane has solid proof of this or if it's just wishful thinking.

"I know what you're thinking but hear me out." He holds his hands up defensively, his face serious. "Everything was fine between them, until my dad got burned really bad doing some stunt on a movie set. He had to get skin grafts and crap—it was pretty gross. Anyway, I heard my mom begging him to quit and find a safer job. But Dad couldn't do that, stunts are a part of who he is. There were a lot of nights of arguing, always about the same thing. They never knew I was listening. A couple months later they told me Dad was moving out."

"Wow."

"Yeah, and every time Dad comes to pick me up, they almost act like they're still married. And I'm pretty sure neither has dated anyone else."

"Do you hope they'll get back together?"

He shrugs. "I've kind of given up hope on that. This all happened when I was ten. Anyway, it's getting late. We should probably find Abigail and Mark, huh?"

I check the clock on my phone, realizing I'm probably going to be late for my meds. I mentally shrug, oh well. An hour late probably won't kill me. Though my mother might.

Kane stands, then offers me his hand. I give him a small smile and accept his help.

We head back toward the boardwalk, listening to the sounds of the waves crashing on the beach, gulls calling, and people talking and laughing. It's nice. It's normal. It's something I haven't allowed myself since my diagnosis.

"You up for some In-N-Out Burger?" Kane asks.

"I would *kill* for some In-N-Out Burger," I confess, my stomach grumbling.

Kane pulls his phone from the pocket of his cargo shorts and quickly shoots off a text. The phone is buzzing with a reply before he can even put it away.

"Abigail says to meet her down by the water. She's trying to flag down Mark."

"Wait, he's *still* surfing?" I ask in surprise.

"Oh yeah, his endurance is ridiculous. It can be really annoying sometimes. He literally only comes to shore every couple hours to chug water and maybe cram down a protein bar, then he's back out there."

I shake my head. "Why do you guys come to the beach with him if he ditches you to surf?"

"Because," Kane says, as if it should be obvious. As if that single non-answer is an answer.

I think back to my old friends. There's no way they would have sat on the beach while I surfed for hours. They would've ditched me after ten minutes. Well, maybe not Rachel. I push her from my mind, not wanting to think about her betrayal, and return my attention to the present. "You're a good friend," I tell him. "You and Abigail both."

Kane beams and slings his arm around my shoulders again. I don't stop him, though I do wonder if I'm leading him on. I don't want to get romantically involved with anyone. I can't. It isn't fair for anyone else to have to deal with me and my medical issues. I especially don't want to burden someone like Kane.

"Did you know I used to be next door neighbors with Mark?"

I shake my head no.

"When my parents got divorced, Mom and I had to move. Abigail's family bought my old house. She actually has my old bedroom."

"That must be weird," I say.

Kane shrugs. "It was at first. I was actually really jealous because suddenly Mark was hanging out with Abigail more than me. I was ten, and Mom wouldn't let me ride my bike all the way over to Mark's any time I wanted. Eventually Mark made me hang out with both of them, and we've been like family ever since. It's actually nice to get to visit my old house pretty much whenever I want." He pauses. "There's Abigail."

We spot her standing at the water's edge. The waves lap her bare feet, as she flails her arms in the air like a maniac. I follow her gaze into the ocean and spy a surfer riding to shore. As the wave gives out, he drops to his stomach on the board and paddles. Abigail drops her arms to her sides and turns to us.

"Hey," she says.

"How long have you been standing here?" Kane asks. Something about the way he's grinning tells me this is nothing new.

Abigail rolls her eyes. "A good five minutes. I'm sure he saw me right away, but you know Mark."

Mark jogs in from the ocean moments later, board under his arm and water dripping from his brown hair. He's grinning. "Killer waves today, guys," he says, looking from Abigail to Kane. His eyes fall on me, "Oh, hey, Summer."

I give him a small wave. "Hey."

"In-N-Out Burger," Kane says. "Let's go."

"Yeah, yeah, hang tight, man." Mark walks away from us toward the on site showers to rinse the salty ocean spray and sand from his body. We trail behind, waiting as he stands under the spray and peels off his wetsuit to reveal a pair of compression shorts beneath. I blush and avert my eyes. Mark is fit, and those shorts leave almost nothing to the imagination. Who knew he was rocking those abs under his baggy t-shirts and shorts.

I catch Kane frowning at Mark, and then he glances at me. I pretend to be busy digging in my purse. I pull out a tube of lip balm and smear it on my lips while I look out at the waves.

"I know, right?" Abigail whispers conspiratorially to me. "It's hard for any straight girl not to stare."

"Can we go yet?" Kane complains.

Abigail steps away from me, and out of the corner of my eye, I see her hand Mark a towel. One by one, she passes him clothes and a pair of sandals. I count to thirty before turning back, assuming it's safe to look again.

Mark is now clad in a pair of shorts and is pulling a faded red t-shirt over his head. He slips his feet into the athletic sandals and waves for us to follow him back to his car. Abigail rides shotgun, leaving the backseat for Kane and me.

I'm glad to see that Mark is a careful driver, pulling out cautiously and using his indicator. The trio chats during the ten minute drive, while I'm content to sit and silently listen.

When we arrive, Mark holds the restaurant door open for Abigail, then Kane grabs it. Mark shakes his head and walks in.

Kane grins and gestures for me to enter before him. This feels oddly like a double date, though I'm pretty sure Abigail and Mark aren't together. Plus, this isn't a date with Kane...at least, I don't think it is.

We place our orders at the counter and, after the ice cream earlier today, I'm not surprised when Kane pays for my meal. Maybe this *is* a date? I'm not sure how I feel about *that*, though I am having a fun time with him.

We fill our cups at the drink station while our food is being prepared, then return to the counter to wait. Kane grabs the tray with my food and his, while Abigail grabs the other with hers and Mark's.

We find a booth, and Abigail and Mark sit on one side, leaving me to slide in next to Kane on the other. He casually puts his arm around my shoulders, and I suppress a smile.

I catch Mark smirking at Kane, shaking his head slightly.

Kane ignores him and focuses on Abigail. "So, tonight's the big sleepover. What's on the agenda? Pillow fights? Talking about boys? Braiding each other's hair?"

"Wow, Kane," Abigail says with a roll of her eyes. "Could your idea of a sleepover be any more antiquated?"

"Antiquated. Big word, Abz." Kane grins, then dodges the fry Abigail lobs at him.

I watch their easy banter and envy the friendship these three share. Rachel and I used to be this close. *Before.*

"But really, what *are* you doing tonight?" Kane asks before taking a giant bite of his burger. Ketchup drips down the side of his mouth, and I grimace.

Mark is shaking his head again, chewing a bite of his own burger, his face still clean.

"You're disgusting, Kane," Abigail says.

Kane shrugs and continues chewing.

"I'm not sure what's on the agenda. Summer?"

Three pairs of eyes settle on me, waiting for an answer. "Oh, um…" I take a long sip from my Coke to buy time, my mind whirring. I wasn't even sure Abigail would agree to this. Was I supposed to schedule an evening of activities? I never had to do that with Rachel. "Watch movies? Hang out?"

"There you have it. Movies and hanging out. Happy?" Abigail says, waving a fry at Kane. He reaches out and snatches it from her fingers, popping it into his mouth.

"What are you doing tonight?" I ask, shifting the focus.

"Hanging out at Mark's house," Kane says automatically.

Mark's eyebrows rise. "Did Mark know about this?"

I hold back a laugh.

Kane grins. "He does now."

It comes as no surprise that my mother is waiting in the foyer when Abigail and I arrive. The front door swings open before we even reach the top step.

"You must be Abigail!" Mom says, a huge smile on her face. "I'm Summer's mom, Susan."

I suppress a groan. Could she *be* any more embarrassing?

"Thanks for letting me sleep over," Abigail says with a smile.

"Any time." Mom motions us inside. "Come on in, girls, I've got dinner going, should be ready any minute."

"Actually, Mom, we just ate."

"Oh." Mom sounds disappointed.

"We're going to hang out in my room for a while, okay?"

"Okay, but Summer don't forget—"

"I know, Mom!" I cut her off before she can spill the beans about my meds in front of Abigail.

Mom's lips press into a thin line, and she lets the reminder go unsaid, as she closes the front door. I lead Abigail upstairs to my bedroom.

Safe in the confines of my room, I shut the door behind us and face Abigail. "Sorry, my mom is..." I trail off. I can't finish that sentence without sounding like a spoiled, ungrateful brat.

Abigail is busy looking around my room. "Don't worry about it. Your mom seems nice."

"Yeah."

A high-pitched voice screeches, "Boo!" and I jump.

My sister jumps out from behind my bed, and I lunge for her. "Mandy!"

She ducks out of reach and runs for the door, slipping out of sight. I turn back to Abigail, a scowl on my face.

"And that's my little sister."

Abigail laughs. "She seems like fun."

I roll my eyes. "Sure. Fun. If you like someone sneaking into your bedroom and messing with your stuff all the time."

She shrugs. "I have older brothers. I was the one sneaking into bedrooms and messing with stuff."

We both laugh. I perch on the end of my bed, my heart rate finally slowing from the scare Mandy gave me.

"You have a *lot* of makeup," Abigail says, standing in front of my vanity. All of my brushes are lined up beside various tubes of lipstick, palettes of eyeshadow, and pretty much everything else you can imagine. Abigail reaches out and grabs an eyeliner, reading the label. "I've had my eye on this one for a while. How do you like it?"

I suddenly remember Kane mentioning Abigail and her eyeliner. Maybe we have something in common after all.

"It's all right, not worth the price, though." I open the top vanity drawer and pull out another eyeliner. "This one is much better. Glides on super smooth and lasts for hours with no smudging."

Abigail takes the stick from me and pulls out her phone. She snaps a photo. "I'll have to check this one out."

"It's nice to hang out with someone who appreciates makeup as much as I do."

She laughs. "Are you kidding? I hang out with *Mark and Kane* most of the time. They don't know the difference between eyeliner and mascara."

"You don't have any girl friends?"

She pauses, and I wonder if I've offended her. "Let's just say that most girls are...intimidated by me."

My brow furrows. "Okay..."

Abigail grows quiet, and an awkward silence falls between us. I scramble for another topic, any topic at all. What comes out of my mouth is, "So, are you and Mark together?"

Abigail laughs. "God, no. Mark is like a brother."

"Oh." I feel a fierce blush creep into my cheeks. "And Kane?"

"*So* not my type."

"What is your type?"

Her eyes skim me up and down. "Not male."

My eyes grow wide in surprise. "Oh."

Abigail gives me a wry smile. "Now you see why a lot of girls don't want to be friends with me. They think I'm going to hit on them or something." She picks up a tube of lipstick, removes the cap, and inspects the color.

"That's dumb."

"Tell me about it." Silence falls between us once more, then she says, "Ready to cancel this sleepover yet?"

"That depends."

Abigail raises her brows. "On?"

"Am I your type?"

Abigail grins. "You're too innocent for me."

I laugh, relieved. "Then no."

"Good." She smiles. "I think we could be good friends, Summer."

I return the smile. I hope she's right.

As our sleepover progresses, I silently thank my parents for pushing the sleepover issue. Abigail is a lot of fun. She's quick to make jokes, and we like a lot of the same movies. After sneaking down to the kitchen for my meds and a pile of snacks, I return to my room. We put on a mid 2000's rom-com and paint our nails while we talk.

"So, what do you think of Kane?" Abigail asks.

"He's nice," I say automatically.

Abigail rolls her eyes. "He might be the nicest guy you'll ever meet."

"Really?" That's high praise, but considering what I know of Kane, not surprising.

"Kane is like a puppy. He's quick to give away his loyalty and sometimes too trusting." She gives me a pointed look. "I like you, Summer, but I've been friends with Kane for years. I'm sure you've already realized this, but he doesn't just like you, he *like* likes you. Please, don't break him."

"I promise, I have no intention of breaking him."

"Don't lead him on either. If you don't *like him* like him, you've got to let him know. Soon."

I swallow hard. How did I end up having this conversation?

13

KANE

I love my house but hanging out at Mark's is the best. As the youngest of five kids—with an eleven-year gap between kid four and Mark—he's sort of raised himself. I'll never say it out loud, but I think by the time Mark was born, his parents were done with the whole parenting thing.

When we were little, Mark spent a lot of time at my house while his parents were gone. His siblings did a lot of babysitting, but it wasn't long before they moved on to college and then real life. After I moved, and Abigail moved into my old house, she sort of took over keeping Mark company when I couldn't. Now that we're older, his house has become our central hangout. We can do pretty much anything we want because his parents are rarely home. Abigail jokes that Mark's parents got lucky with him. If *I* was their kid, they wouldn't be able to get away with leaving me alone so often. Or ever. The cast on my wrist tells me she's probably right.

As usual, Mark's parents are gone. I think he said something about them being in Paris for their anniversary. Or was it Venice? Whatever, somewhere in Europe, so we have free reign of the house tonight.

I rummage through the film collection in Mark's den. Shoving aside movie after movie, I search for what I'm sure I've seen here before.

We dropped Summer and Abigail off twenty minutes ago, and already I'm preparing for my next plan of action as far as Summer is concerned.

"Seriously dude, what are you doing? My mom will kill me if you don't put those back exactly as you found them."

He's exaggerating, I think, but I start gathering the DVD's I've scattered on the floor around me. "There's no way these were organized before I got my hands on them," I say.

Mark doesn't reply, he's lounging on the couch, engrossed in something on his phone, which is fine, because I'm on a mission.

"Ah-ha!" I hold up a DVD case triumphantly.

Mark glances up from his phone and cocks an eyebrow at the movie in my hand. "*Say Anything?* Really? If you want an old movie, I'm pretty sure my dad has *Die Hard* and *Back to the Future*."

"This is research." I pull the disc out of the case and pop it into the DVD player.

"Do I even want to know?"

"This is Summer's favorite movie. She says it's romantic." I point at Mark. "*Research.*"

"Whatever, man. Just don't expect me to pay attention."

I ignore him and press play, then take a seat in the recliner.

When the movie ends, Mark is fast asleep on the couch, his mouth gaping open. I smirk at him and decide this would be the perfect opportunity to see how many cotton balls I can shove into his mouth without waking him. I move to ease the footrest on my recliner closed but press too hard and it slams shut. Mark startles awake, and his phone slides from his chest to the floor.

So much for my prank. I get up to retrieve the disc from the player.

"So, how was the *research*," Mark asks with a yawn.

Shoving the DVD case back on the shelf, I turn and face him. "I don't get it."

"Get what?"

"The whole thing."

Mark laughs. "Don't ask me."

"But I liked the part where he shows up at her house and holds the old radio up outside her bedroom window."

"Save this conversation for Summer, dude."

I shut up. I didn't expect Mark to want to talk about the movie anyway. I mean, he slept through most of it.

"I'm bored." I break the silence.

"Wanna play Xbox?"

"Sure. Even though you *always* win."

"Not my fault you're so bad at video games."

I sock him playfully in the arm, well, mostly playfully, and hand him a controller.

We spend the rest of the evening playing games. Mark wins every time, of course.

If *Say Anything* has taught me anything it's that I need to step up my game. I'm not sure how though.

I crash on Mark's couch for the night and he drops me off at home late the next morning.

When I walk in the front door, I hear Mom humming to herself. I dump my bag and skateboard on the floor in the entryway and follow the sounds to the kitchen.

"Hey, Mom." I casually lean against the counter and watch as she mixes up a bowl of chicken salad.

"Hey, hon." She smiles at me, then continues mixing. "How was the beach yesterday? I see you didn't break anything."

I chuckle, then reach out and dip my finger in the chicken salad, scooping up a glob and popping it into my mouth. She hits my hand with the spoon when I go for seconds.

"The beach was good," I say.

"Just *good*? You're not going to regale me with tales of your adventures?" She sets the spoon in the bowl and gives me her full attention. "What's up?"

"Mom, how do I get a girl to like me?"

She pauses, blinking, as she silently studies my face. "That's a very open question. I'm not sure how to answer." She purses her lips. "Who's the girl?"

"Summer," I say. "The girl from that last visit to urgent care."

"Ahh." A slow smile spreads across her lips.

"You've *got* to help me, Mom. I've asked her out twice, and she fed me some line about not dating anyone right now." I roll my eyes. "But she came to the beach with us yesterday and we hung out for hours. She's so easy to talk to, and I think she had a good time with me."

"You should respect her wishes. Be her friend, but don't force yourself at her."

"But Mom, I really, *really* like her. She's my partner in foods class, so we've hung out a couple times, and she's so nice and fun and pretty."

"Well," she pauses, lost in thought. "Show her I raised you to be chivalrous and respectful. It's the little things that really add up. Opening doors for her, offering to carry her backpack, those kinds of things."

I can totally handle that. "Thanks, Mom." I give her a kiss on the cheek, while stealing another finger scoop of chicken salad. She smacks me in the arm, and I race from the kitchen.

An hour later, inspiration strikes. What's more chivalrous than gift giving? I turn off the TV I've been watching and shout to Mom, "I'm heading out for a bit. Back soon!"

Mom calls back a farewell from her office down the hall.

I stop short when I reach the entryway. Mom must have confiscated my board again while I was in front of the TV. I should have hidden it in my room, maybe she would have forgotten. Probably not.

I pull my bike from the garage and pedal through the streets of Sol del Mar, until I end up at the Ocean View Market. It's a misleading name, because there are about six blocks of residential houses and apartments separating the store from the sea. There's a chance you can see the ocean from the roof, but I've never had the opportunity to find out. Like most locals, I like to shop at the OVM because it's far enough from the boardwalk that tourists don't usually wander in.

Entering the store, I head straight for the snack and candy aisle near the back. I have to squeeze past a group of girls who probably go to my school, and eventually I find the gummy bears.

"Isn't that the guy Summer's been hanging with?" I hear one girl say in a hushed voice.

"I swear I saw them getting ice cream at the beach yesterday," another girl says. There's a chorus of shushing and more giggles.

I strain my ears to hear more, but there's no need, because from the corner of my eye I catch one of the girls approaching on my left.

"Hey."

Glancing up from the candy, I recognize the girl from school. She's short, with long, silky black hair and dark almond eyes. Her lids are painted sparkly pink and she's smiling.

"Hey," I echo, then wait for her to continue.

"We couldn't help but notice that Summer Swanson has been hanging with you at school. We were just wondering...are you guys a thing?"

I blink. "A thing?"

"You know, are you dating?"

"Oh. Uh, no," I admit. I wish I could tell her I *was* dating Summer, but that would be a lie. "We're just friends."

"Oh." She looks at the floor. I wonder why she sounds so disappointed. "Okay, sorry to bug you."

"Wait, what's your name?"

Her eyes meet mine again. "Rachel Yang."

"I'm Kane."

"I know," she says. "We have foods class together."

So that's where I've seen her.

"Right," I say. "I knew that." I so didn't know that. It's hard for me to pay attention to anything else when Summer is around.

"See you around." Rachel gives a little wave, then returns to her friends. They converge on her, like a pack of hyenas on a carcass.

14

SUMMER

Abigail's little speech is on my mind all Sunday. I envy the friendship she shares with Kane and Mark. She's given me a lot to think about.

Kane likes me—a lot. And the more time I spend with him, the more I like him too. He's funny and sweet and deserves someone far less complicated than me. I shouldn't be with anyone, but especially not someone so good. It's not fair to him. *Especially* since I'm not about to tell him exactly *how* broken I am. The last thing I want is to be labeled The Sick Girl.

My emotions wage war all day and night. It's like the hamster in my brain, running on its little wheel, is on some kind of drug. Unable to stop or even slow down. Sleep, which is hard to come by on my best nights, is non-existent.

When morning comes, I'm already short on spoons. I'm both mentally and physically exhausted. I've gone back and forth in my head; give this thing with Kane a chance or end things before he has a chance to really get hurt.

Standing in the lunch line at school, I finally decide to let him down easy. Before he becomes too invested in the idea of a relationship with me.

As I exit the lunch line, my gaze falls upon my old lunch table in the cafeteria. Rachel is there, talking animatedly with Avery and Madison from the volleyball team. Rachel seems to feel my eyes on her, and she looks up. Our eyes meet, and I hurry out of the cafeteria, nearly bumping into Kane at the door in my mad dash to escape my past.

Kane grins and reaches out to steady my lunch tray.

"Hey," he says, taking the tray from my hands. He adjusts the backpack hanging from his right shoulder. "Let me."

"Oh," I say in surprise. Dammit, how can I break the news to him when he's being so sweet? "Thank you."

"No problem." Kane begins walking, and the corner of my mouth twitches up. We reach the door to the courtyard, and he pushes it open with his back, holding it to allow me through first. "You're sitting with us again, right?"

I nod, because my other option is going back to sitting alone. After being accepted by Kane's friends, I've realized I don't want to go back. That makes my decision to stop things before they start even more difficult.

Kane leads me to the table where Mark is already sitting and sets the tray down.

I sit, and Kane takes his place beside me and across from Mark, whose attention is fixed somewhere behind us.

"Earth to Mark." Kane waves his hand in front of Mark's face to get his attention.

Mark stares at Kane, blank faced for a moment, and says nothing before taking a bite of his pizza.

Averting my eyes, I focus on my own slice. Grimacing, I place one of my napkins over the cheese and soak up as much of the excess grease as I can. My doctor has advised me to avoid food like this, but I'm not ready to give up this little piece of normalcy. I remove the disgusting napkin and take a bite of the pizza; it's not quite hot, but it *is* tasty.

"So, how was your big sleepover?" Kane asks me.

Before I can answer, Abigail appears behind him. Glaring, she whacks him in the back of the head with her knuckles.

"I told you, Kane, sleepovers are sacred. What happens at the sleepover, *stays* at the sleepover."

"Jeez, Abz." He rubs the back of his head. "Use your words. And it's a sleepover, not *Fight Club*."

She takes her seat across from me and sticks her tongue out at Kane.

I take pity on him. "We had a fun time."

Kane glances at Abigail, then turns his attention back to me. "Good. I'm glad you two are hitting it off. One more excuse to hang out with us after this term ends."

"One *more* reason?" Mark asks, eyebrows raised. I hadn't even realized he was paying attention.

"Obviously I'm *número uno*." Kane shoots him a cheeky grin.

I shift in my seat beside him. Kane's personality is overwhelming at times. What must it be like to be so open with your feelings all the time?

"What's the plan for after school?" Kane asks.

"Homework," Abigail says with a groan. "If I don't ace my bio test my parents will murder me, and I'll never get into Santa Barbara's marine biology program."

I'm impressed that Abigail wants to be a marine biologist. That would be a really cool job. I used to have plans for after high school...until my disease.

"Mark?" Kane directs his attention at him.

Mark shrugs.

Finally, he looks at me. "And you?"

"Oh, um..." I look between Kane's friends. When my eyes meet Abigail's, I can see her mentally reminding me of our conversation. My mouth feels dry, and I have to swallow before answering. "I was planning to just go home. Do homework. Catch up on sleep."

"Did Abz keep you up all night?" Kane winks at Abigail. "I hear she really saws logs."

Abigail shoots him a glare. "You're lucky I don't have french fries, mister, because if I did, there would be a handful of them heading toward you right now."

Kane laughs and holds his hands up in surrender. He turns back to me. "Can I get you to reconsider? I wanted to show you something cool."

Out of the corner of my eye I catch Abigail rolling her eyes. She's also smiling though.

"Something cool?" I ask.

"Something *very* cool. I promise."

I pull my lower lip between my teeth. I really should say no. I really do need to catch up on sleep, but he seems so excited. Abigail is right, Kane *is* just like a puppy; it's impossible to tell him no. I feel like I'm going to regret this, but I say, "Okay."

The grin on Kane's face is infectious, and I find myself smiling back. I *really* hope I don't regret this.

Kane and I walk to our foods class together, and we take our seats. Instead of Kane's usual talking non-stop routine, he's staring at something behind me, a quizzical expression on his face.

I narrow my eyes. "What are you staring at?"

He shakes his head and points behind me.

Turning in my seat, I look in the direction he's pointing. All I see is the clock on the classroom wall, telling us there's one minute until class begins. I turn back, ready to tell him I don't see anything, when I realize there's a bag of gummy bears sitting on the table in front of me.

I open my mouth, then close it. Looking at Kane, I realize what just happened. He's grinning from ear to ear.

"I'm so glad you fell for that," he says, chuckling.

I roll my eyes, but there's no suppressing the smile on my face. "What's this for?"

"You said they were your favorite."

Glancing around the room for Ms. Knope, I open the bag and offer him one.

"Thanks," he says.

"No, thank you." I select three reds from the bag, and one by one bite off their heads before eating the rest of their bodies.

"Do you only eat the red ones?" he asks, watching me with interest.

Shaking my head, I say, "I know it's weird, but I like to eat them one color at a time, going in rainbow order."

He laughs, and I see a few heads turn in our direction.

Ms. Knope stands from her desk, and I quickly shove the bag of candy in my three-ring binder. Kane's hand snakes out and reaches into the binder, swiping one more from the bag. "Sorry, it's an orange," he whispers before popping it into in his mouth.

Why did he have to buy me my favorite snack? Kane is making it really difficult for me to turn him down.

When school ends, I head to the bike racks to meet Kane. He isn't there yet, but I recognize his blue bike and lean against the rack. I don't have to wait long before he comes walking out the front door and toward me.

"So, you *do* know how to walk through the halls." I feel like an idiot as soon as the words leave my lips. Hopefully he remembers what I said the last time he asked to meet me here.

He laughs and unchains his bike. "Don't tell my friends, it's a secret."

"I've got a question," I say, as he mounts the bike.

"Shoot."

"Do all your shirts feature food puns?"

He glances down at his t-shirt—which reads "Don't Go Bacon My Heart"—then beams at me. "Only my favorites."

I shake my head and climb on the handlebars, wearing my backpack on my chest like last time. "Remember, you break me, I kill you."

"It would be a crime to break someone like you, Summer."

A feeling of warmth erupts in my stomach, and even though he can't see my face, I try not to smile.

Kane keeps his daredevil ways in check as he pedals away from school. I ask him for a hint, but he tells me it's top secret. When he finally stops the bike, we're at the beach.

"Um..." I say, climbing down from the handlebars and looking around. "This is the really cool thing you wanted to show me?" It looks exactly the same as it had on Saturday, except with fewer people crowding the boardwalk and beach.

"This is just part one." He chains his bike to the rack and takes my hand in his. I stare for a moment at our intertwined fingers, his warm hand so much larger than mine. His tan skin is a stark contrast to my own complexion, which has paled from avoiding the sun as much as possible since spring.

I know I should stop this, end things now before we get in too deep...But it's been so long since I've let anyone in. And it feels nice. So I let him hold my hand, and I try to convince myself it means nothing; I can stop this at any time. But I have butterflies in my stomach, and I think deep down I know I'm lying to myself.

Kane gives my hand a squeeze and leads me down the board-walk. I look around, anywhere but at him. The guilt is gnawing at me for allowing myself this little piece of happiness, when I know it will only end in heartbreak for him. I'm irreparably broken, and he doesn't know what he's getting into.

But I do.

My gaze is fixed on the rhythmic crashing of the waves on the sand, when Kane stops. I look to the other side of the boardwalk and realize we've stopped in front of one of those cheesy tourist kiosks selling airbrushed t-shirts and hats.

"Is *this* the really cool thing?" I ask skeptically. As a kid, I begged my parents for an airbrushed t-shirt with my name on it. They gave in, and after only a couple of times wearing it, it lay forgotten in the bottom of my dresser drawer.

"Shh," he says, grinning at me. He turns his attention to the guy sitting behind the kiosk and whispers something in his ear.

The guy laughs and nods. "Yeah, I can do that."

"Do what?" I ask, stepping closer to watch. The guy grabs a plain white t-shirt from under the kiosk and sets up to begin airbrushing. I watch, fascinated, as an image comes to life before us. I laugh when I realize it's a taco. Kane nudges me with his elbow, and I look up at him and grin. When the guy is done with the shirt, there's an image of a sad cartoon taco and the words, "I Don't Wanna Taco 'Bout It" in cheesy black and purple airbrush writing.

"What do you think?" Kane asks, gesturing to the shirt.

I inspect the work of art; it's hilarious. "I don't think it'll fit you," I finally say.

He laughs. "That's okay. It's for you."

My mouth falls open. "For me?"

He nods. "I think you need to experience the joys of food pun t-shirts. What better way than to start with an airbrushed taco pun?"

I shake my head, but I'm grinning as Kane pays the man, who says to come back in about a half hour to pick up the shirt.

Kane takes my hand in his again, and we continue down the boardwalk. We reach the end, near the rocky cliff where we sat and ate ice cream just days ago. Kane leads me off the boardwalk, where the sand turns to rock.

"Where are we going?"

"You'll see when we get there. You'll love it."

"Love it more than my very own taco shirt?"

"*Dang*, I knew that would be a tough act to follow."

I laugh. Talking to Kane is easy...too easy. After a few minutes of walking, he leads me down a rocky slope.

I eye the slope skeptically; It's steep and littered with loose rocks. I'm tired from my sleepless night, the long day of school, and the walk this far. But I force myself to push forward. I want to see what the big secret is.

We pick our way carefully across the terrain, but I step on a loose rock and my sneaker slides. Kane reacts quickly, grasping my arm in his uninjured hand before I can slide more than a couple inches. For as accident prone as Kane seems to be, he has good reflexes—at least as far as my safety is concerned.

"Thanks." I brush my hair from my face and try to slow my heart, racing from the near fall or his close proximity I can't say.

"I told you I wouldn't break you," he says. His face is serious. It's rare to see this side of Kane. I like the goofy Kane but seeing this side of him is a rare moment to be treasured.

"We're almost there." He releases his grip on my arm and takes my hand. We continue carefully down the slope and come out on a stretch of perfect, white sand beach next to a lagoon. The turquoise water glints in the sunlight, and I feel like we've been transported to a private, tropical island. I've never seen anything this beautiful before.

"Wow." I'm breathless, and not just from trying not to slide down the steep incline. "I've been to this beach a thousand times, but I never even knew this place existed." I try to memorize every detail of this tiny slice of paradise, from the glittering sand beneath our feet littered in shells and the occasional piece of sea glass, to the stretch of blue beyond, shifting from turquoise to cerulean to cobalt and every shade in between.

"Most people don't look past the cliffside, they seem to think the beach ends there. And those who do look, most aren't brave enough to make that climb down." From the corner of my eye, I notice him studying me, as if I'm more interesting than the beautiful scene spread around us.

"You're definitely not most people," I murmur, more to myself than to him.

"Hey, Summer?"

"Hmm?" I give him my full attention and realize he's only inches away from me.

"Thanks for letting me show you this place."

"No, thank *you*."

He smiles again, and I feel the corners of my mouth tug up in return. And then he's coming closer, his face slowly moving toward mine, angling just a bit to the side, and I freeze.

I know what's coming, and I know I should stop it, but I don't. Stopping him would ruin this beautiful, perfect moment. So I let him come closer, and when his lips meet mine, the butterflies I felt earlier take flight, and I wonder why I ever doubted this.

I kiss him back.

I allow myself to forget about all my problems. For just this moment, I'm a normal seventeen-year-old girl being kissed by the boy she likes.

15

———

KANE

Summer's lips are soft and warm against mine. I'm so glad I took the chance and kissed her. For a second, I think she might push me away, but she doesn't. I can feel the exact moment when she leans into the kiss, the barrier between us crumbling. It's better than the time I finally nailed my first ollie on my skateboard.

When we separate, I can't help but grin like the Cheshire Cat. I just kissed Summer Swanson. And, even better, she kissed me back.

She looks down at our feet, pushing a strand of hair behind her ear, and tries to hide her own smile. I'm not fooled. She likes me. Summer Swanson *actually* likes me.

"So," I say. "Are you ready to pick up your shirt, or should we stay a little longer." I cross my fingers behind my back and silently chant, *stay, stay, stay*.

She swallows but remains silent for a beat. Finally, she says, "Let's stay."

She doesn't have to say it twice. I take her hand and tug gently so that we're both sitting in the soft sand, the cliffside casting shade over us. I don't release her hand, letting our fingers twine together, and I gently squeeze. I can't stop the smile that's fixed on my face, and why would I? I'm so happy right now, I want to shout it from the rooftops.

Except, now I don't know what to say to her. Only Summer has the power to shut me up. I've never been at a loss for words, ask anyone.

Fortunately, Summer breaks the silence. "Now what?" she asks. Her voice is soft and hesitant.

"What do you mean?" I turn my head and face her. She's staring out at the ocean.

She shrugs and remains silent. The hand that isn't holding mine scoops a handful of sand and lets it trickle through her fingers.

I furrow my brow, my smile fading. Is she having second thoughts? "Well," I begin, then pause while I figure out exactly what to say. "I like you, Summer. I want to get to know you better." Unable to help myself, I add, "And I wouldn't mind kissing you again."

Her hand stills, half submerged in the sand, and a small smile forms on her lips. She shakes her head slowly, and I'm afraid she's going to tell me this was a mistake. That she never should have kissed me back. That we should forget it ever happened.

But she doesn't. She turns her head and looks me in the eye. "Okay."

"Okay?" I know my voice is far too eager, but I can't help it. My gaze locks on her beautiful blue eyes, willing this to be reality.

"Okay," she confirms. "Let's give this a try."

I pump my fist in a *nailed it* gesture and fall back in the sand. Summer laughs, then lays back beside me.

"Want to go to the homecoming dance with me?" I ask her.

She pulls her lower lip between her teeth, lost in thought. Hesitantly, she says, "Okay."

"Cool. And would it be okay for me to kiss you again?"

She shakes her head, laughing, and says, "You ask the second time, but not the first?"

"If I'd asked the first time you might have said no. The moment was perfect, I didn't want to ruin it." I pause, studying her expression. "Did I just ruin this moment?"

She doesn't use her words, instead she sits up and leans down toward me, closing the gap between us. She presses her lips to mine, and when we part, she lays down again, and I slip my arm under her head, pulling her close. I shut my eyes and grin.

"Best day ever," I mutter under my breath. Her body shakes with silent laughter beside me.

We stay like that for a while, listening to the calming melody of the ocean lapping the shore and feeling the salty sea breeze caress our skin. I'd be happy to stay like this forever, nestled in the soft, warm bed of sand with Summer in my arms, but I know I need to get her home.

"I bet that shirt is ready," I say, breaking the comfortable silence we've been laying in.

"I bet that shirt has been ready for an hour," she agrees. She shifts, preparing to push herself to sitting. I quickly sit up and position myself so I'm hovering half above her, my face inches away, blocking her from moving.

"Before I let you up, are you going to let me take you to dinner and a movie?" I ask. I keep my expression sincere, hoping she realizes I'm serious about this.

"What if I say no?" Her expression is blank, face unreadable, and I really hope she's messing with me right now.

"I'll have to hold your new shirt hostage until you agree."

"Well, we can't have that, can we?" The corner of her lip twitches up, and a wave of relief washes over me. She *was* messing with me.

"No, we can't. I shelled out the big bucks for you to enter the wonderful world of food pun t-shirts."

"Are you sure I'm ready?" Her voice is saturated in mock sincerity, but the wide grin on her face gives her away. It's the smile I love seeing, the one she doesn't show nearly enough. She's holding nothing back now, and I'm falling more in love with her every time she opens her mouth to speak.

"I have faith in you, Grasshopper." I quickly lean down and give her a peck on the lips, then sit up. I offer her my non-cast-covered hand and help her stand. Still holding hands, we hike up the steep incline, then down the rocky path back to the boardwalk.

We stop by the kiosk and grab the shirt, which despite my insistence, she refuses to put on. I carry the bag for her as we walk back toward my bike. This isn't the first time I've held her hand, but this time feels different—better—now that she's agreed to go out with me.

We near the volleyball nets, and Rachel approaches us.

"Hey, Summer," she says. Her voice is hesitant, and I wonder why. Her gaze lingers on Summer's hand in mine, and she adds, "Hey, Kane."

Summer is frozen beside me, still silent as the dead. I step in and say, "Hey, how's it going?"

"Good," she says, brushing a strand of black hair behind her ear. "Nice night for the beach, right?" Her gaze darts to my and Summer's hands again, then back to our faces.

I'm suddenly very aware of Summer's hand in mine; she's squeezing so tight I'm losing feeling. Why hasn't she said anything? I swear I've seen these two in the halls together in the past. I thought they were friends.

"Sure," I say. Summer remains a statue beside me.

Rachel nods, looking between the two of us. "Anyway...I just wanted to say hi." She shifts her weight from one foot to the other, then casts a glance over her shoulder. The same group of girls from Ocean View Market are watching from a distance.

"Bye." The one word from Summer is as icy as winter in

Antarctica. I'm stunned. What could have happened between these girls for Summer to be so cold?

Rachel mutters a goodbye and retreats to the safety of her waiting friends. I glance at Summer, trying to read her expression and figure out what she's feeling and what's going through her head right now.

"Come on," I say, pumping my voice full of enthusiasm. I want to get her mind off this strange encounter and cheer her up. I gently squeeze her hand. She looks at our claspsed hands in surprise, finally relaxing her fingers. Could it be that she hadn't even realized how tight her grip was?

I take a step, and she follows my lead. When we reach the bike rack, I tell her, "I know. If I break you, you kill me."

She finally smiles again, but it's fainter than before, as though the brief conversation with Rachel has drained her. I mount the bike, slipping the bag with her shirt onto one handlebar, and she climbs aboard. The ride to her house is slow and quiet, the only conversation is her telling me where to turn. When we arrive and she climbs off, I lean my bike against her garage door and walk her to the front door.

"See you tomorrow?"

She nods. "Yeah."

I quickly duck my head forward and give her our fourth kiss, a quick peck on the lips.

When I pull back there's a small smile on her face. It's clear the Rachel thing—whatever that was—is still bothering her, but at least she's smiling again.

I don't think I've ever ridden my bike so fast in my life. I'm sure I would have set records—if such records existed—crossing the distance from Summer's house to Abigail's.

"Seriously?" Abigail's voice is saturated with incredulity when I tell her and Mark about my amazing afternoon with Summer. I left out the weird Rachel encounter toward the end, I'm still not sure what to make of that.

If I wasn't so ecstatic, Abigail's reaction might annoy me.

"Yes, seriously." I flop back on her bed and try to relive every millisecond of the afternoon on the beach with Summer.

"You really shouldn't kiss and tell," Mark says. He's staring at his phone.

"If I don't talk to you guys about this I might explode."

"Yeah, Mark," Abigail says. "He might explode."

Mark smiles and shakes his head, his eyes never leaving his screen.

"And I for one don't want to have to clean pieces of Kane off my bedroom walls," she adds.

"It was my bedroom first." I snatch a pillow from the bed and hurl it at her. She catches it and throws it back, laughing when it whacks me in the head. I join in her laughter, glad it was just a pillow I threw and not something that could actually cause damage.

"So, you kissed the girl, now what?" Abigail asks.

"Now she's letting me take her out for dinner and a movie..." I trail off before delivering the coupe de grâce. "...and the home-coming dance."

"Nice." Abigail high-fives me. "I hope this works out for you."

"Oh, it will," I say. I'm confident that there's nothing that will come between us now. I can already see our future; college, marriage, and someday kids.

Mark and Abigail exchange a skeptical look, but I ignore them.

"You're not going to make *us* go to the dance too, are you?" Abigail asks, her lip curled up in disgust.

I grin. "It'll be fun. You can be each other's dates."

Mark smirks. "Yeah, sure, whatever."

Abigail groans, and kicks us out soon after, insisting she needs to study. I ride home, still on cloud nine.

I beat Summer to foods class. Our paths haven't crossed yet. It sucks. I wonder where she was at lunch, but I know not to ask questions. She'll tell me if and when she's ready. I just have to be patient.

I watch the door, waiting for her to enter. When she does, a wide grin spreads across my face. Over a long sleeved, light blue top, she's wearing the shirt I got her, in all its airbrushed glory.

"That's a nice shirt," I say as she draws closer.

She sets her bag down and slides into her seat. Shrugging she says, "Some guy at the beach bought it for me."

"Was he hot?" I ask.

She laughs, and a snort escapes, as she tries to muffle it. Her face grows pink, and she lets her hair fall forward to conceal it. Could this girl get any cuter?

"I'm still waiting..." I hedge. She likes me enough to kiss me and agree to go out with me, but I really do wonder if she thinks I'm hot, or at least cute.

She shakes her head, pulling herself together. "He was all right." She tries to act serious, but I can see she's just messing with me.

I scoff. "I bet he was more than all right."

She shrugs again, then says, "Well, he was a pretty good kisser."

My smile at this is so big it's a wonder my face doesn't split in half. "You're not half-bad yourself."

She blushes and hides behind her hair again. I wish she'd stop doing that, I like when she blushes.

"So," I say, stretching my arm out and resting it on the chair back behind her. "About that date you promised..."

"Yes?"

"How about this Friday? You can pick the movie, but I want to pick the restaurant."

"Dare I ask?"

I waggle my eyebrows. "It's a surprise."

"Are we taking your bike?"

I sigh, wondering when this sore subject would come up. "It's that or walking. I kind of don't have my license."

"Oh really?" She raises her eyebrows, a smile tugging at her lips.

I narrow my eyes and glare at my desk. "My mom doesn't seem to trust me behind the wheel."

She snorts again, unsuccessfully trying to hold in her laughter. "I wonder why."

16

SUMMER

This week went by too fast. When Kane dropped me off at home after our private beach excursion, I crashed. Mom woke me for dinner and my meds, and then I was out again. I really shouldn't have gone with him after school. We stayed mostly in the shade, but the sun and all the walking took a toll on me. But all that said, I have no regrets. I know I *should* have regrets, but I think it was worth it.

All week I've eaten lunch with Kane, Abigail, and Mark. It's crazy how quickly they've accepted me as one of them. There's none of the pettiness and gossip that I'm used to from my old friends. It's refreshing. For once, I feel like I can just be me. Well, almost. I may be giving this thing with Kane a shot, but I'm *not* telling him about my illness.

School let out an hour ago, and the weekend has officially begun. I'm supposed to pick up Kane any minute now, but instead I'm staring at my reflection in the full-length mirror on the back of my closet door. Biting my lower lip, I scrutinize my outfit. I don't know why, Kane never cares *what* I wear, but second guessing myself is one of my worst personality traits.

Finally, after applying a fresh coat of lipgloss, I deem myself ready. I'm wearing a baby blue top with a denim skirt. My hair is down around my shoulders, and I have on my favorite silver strappy sandals. It's dressy, but not too dressy. I have no clue what Kane has in mind before our movie.

I drape a white cardigan over my arm and close my bedroom door behind me—a vain attempt to keep Mandy out. It doesn't take long to find Mom, and her car keys, at the kitchen table looking over some legal documents from the office.

"Keys?" I say, holding my hand out toward her.

"Oh, right," Mom says. Absentmindedly, she reaches for the purse sitting on the chair beside her. She extracts the keys and holds them out to me, her focus still on the papers spread out in front of her.

"Thanks, Mom." I turn to leave.

"You look nice."

I freeze, my back to her. I thought I'd get away without her noticing my ensemble.

"Thanks, Mom."

"Who did you say you were meeting?"

My cheeks grow warm as I turn back to face her. "Just...my partner from foods class."

Mom smiles, which makes my face grow warmer. "A *boy*?" There's a teasing quality to her tone of voice.

I roll my eyes and sigh. "Yes, Mother. A boy."

"It's good to see you spending time with friends," Mom says, ignoring the eye roll. "And boys. It's been a while since you've been on a date. You even missed prom."

I fight to keep a scowl off my face, mentally reminding myself that Mom doesn't know how sour the memory of prom is for me.

"Right, well...he's waiting, so..." I wait for her to catch the hint.

"You took your meds, right?" Her voice is serious now.

I nod.

"Go, have fun. Don't stay out too late."

I head for the door and smile when I hear her call out, "Make good choices!"

Closing the door behind me, I leave the comfort of the AC for the warmth of the sun. I climb into the driver's seat of Mom's black SUV, then drive to Kane's house.

I drive slowly, nerves getting the best of me. Only days ago, I had planned to tell him there was no chance for us. Now here I am, pulling into his driveway to pick him up for a date. I pause, mentally preparing myself, before getting out.

How did this happen? How did I end up on a date with Kane Dwyer, or any guy for that matter?

The same thoughts were running through my head a few days ago when he kissed me on my doorstep. I was a flurry of emotions that day, between the kisses, and agreeing to go to the homecoming dance, and of course that awful encounter with Rachel.

By midweek, when I'd finally sorted through everything, I realized that when I'm with Kane I feel more alive than I have in months. With him, I don't feel like I'm at death's door, but like my whole life is ahead of me. What is it about this crazy guy that makes me feel good when nothing else does?

He's the first person I've let in since my life fell apart. When I don't want to talk, he gets it and doesn't push. Kane lets me keep my secrets.

But I wonder, how long will I be able to keep them secret? Sooner or later, I'm bound to have another flare up, and he's going to figure out something is wrong with me. I quickly shove the thought away, determined to live in the here and now.

Breathing deeply, I try to tame my nerves. I stare at Kane's house; it's an unassuming rambler, beige in color with a dark blue door and trim. It's a lot smaller than my own house, but the rock garden in the front yard, dotted with little pops of colorful flowers, indicates it's well cared for.

I debate honking the horn to summon Kane when he doesn't

run outside immediately, but decide against it. That would be an awful first impression if his mom is home.

My god, when did I start caring what his *mother* thinks?

After another deep breath, I step out of the car and stride as confidently as I can toward the front door. I knock twice and wait with my hands clasped together behind my back.

The door opens moments later, and Kane's face lights up at the sight of me.

"Summer, hey!"

His enthusiasm makes me smile. What have I ever done to earn his infatuation?

"Hey. Are you ready?"

"Absolutely. My mom wants to meet you first, though." He turns his head and shouts into the next room, "Ma! She's here!" He turns his attention back to me. "Come on in."

I step through the front door, as Kane's mom enters the room. I vaguely recall her annoyance with Kane at urgent care, and I'm pleased she seems happy to meet me. I suppose meeting Kane's date is less stressful than accruing medical bills for his broken bones.

She smiles at me and extends her hand. I shake it and return the smile.

"You must be the infamous Summer."

I shift my gaze to Kane.

"Mom!" he groans, but he's grinning.

She laughs and wraps an arm around him, pulling him against her in a one-armed hug. I would be mortified if one of my parents did that in front of my date, but Kane just laughs and places his own arm around her.

It's fascinating watching them. Though I've only just met her, I can already see that their relationship is vastly different from mine with my own parents. Maybe because it's just the two of them?

With a laugh, she releases Kane. "What are you kids up to tonight?"

"Dinner and a movie," Kane says.

"And the movie is done at what time?"

Kane groans again, "I don't know, 10:30 or something?"

His mom shakes her head slightly, and I can see she's holding back a smile. "Home by 11:15, got it?" I get the feeling she's not very strict with Kane, and this is just an act to mess with him.

Kane nods.

"Good. You two have fun."

"Bye, Mom!" Kane says, pulling open the front door and taking me by the hand.

"Nice to meet you," I call over my shoulder as I'm ushered outside.

"Sorry about that," Kane says. He doesn't look sorry though. He looks thrilled to have had the chance to show me off.

"Nothing to be sorry about. Your mom seems great."

Kane rushes ahead of me and pulls open the driver's side door for me. I smile in thanks and climb in while he runs around to his side.

"Where to?" I ask, once he's settled beside me.

Kane gives me directions, one street at a time, refusing to tell me the name of our destination. When he finally instructs me to park, we're at a tiny waterfront cafe. It's further south than I usually travel, so I don't recognize it.

"This place has the best enchiladas."

"If you say so."

"I do say so. Come on, you'll love it."

He jumps out of the car, and before I even have my seatbelt unbuckled, he's at my door, opening it for me.

"Thanks," I say, as he extends a hand to help me out.

"My pleasure."

I feel the annoying flush in my cheeks again, and let my hair fall forward to cover it.

"I wish you wouldn't do that." His fingers gently brush my cheek, as he tucks my hair behind one ear, which only causes my cheeks to burn hotter.

"Let's eat," I say quickly, sidestepping him and walking toward the restaurant's front door.

The restaurant has a "seat yourself" sign in the doorway, so we find a booth with a window view that overlooks the ocean. I sit, and instead of seating himself across from me, Kane slides in beside me and picks up a menu. He puts an arm over my shoulder and begins pointing to items on the menu.

"I love their fish tacos," he says.

I wrinkle my nose.

Kane notices and laughs. "Not a fish person?"

"Not really. Most fish are just...too fishy," I say, and instantly regret it. That was so lame.

He laughs. "I think fish are supposed to be fishy." He squeezes my shoulder, then moves down the menu pointing out other entrees he recommends.

We fall back into our usual pattern of Kane cracking jokes and me trying to keep up.

When the server approaches, we order enchiladas, chips and salsa, and soda. The food arrives in record time, and Kane moves to the other side of the booth. I take the initiative and ask him some questions.

"So, your dad is a stuntman?"

Kane nods, his mouth full of food. He swallows and then looks around conspiratorially. "Can you keep a secret?"

Nodding, I almost laugh. I'm the queen of secrets these days.

"I haven't told anyone else this, but I want to be a stuntman like my dad."

"Why am I not surprised?" I'm smiling when I say it, and he grins back.

"When I was little, before the divorce, Mom took me to watch him on set a few times. It was the coolest thing I've ever seen in my entire life. I knew then, that's what I want to do with my life."

"Is that why you're always doing these crazy things?"

He shrugs. "Nah, that's just me."

"So, nobody else knows that you want to be a stuntman?"

He shakes his head.

"Not even Abigail or Mark?"

He shrugs. "They'd probably laugh at me or make a joke. Which is normally cool, but this...well..."

The Kane across the table from me is reminiscent of the serious Kane I'd glimpsed on our walk to the secret beach. I like it. I feel honored that he trusts me enough to keep his secret.

"What about you?" he asks.

17

KANE

W hat *about* me?" Summer asks.

"I just told you my life's ambition, what's yours?"

Her cheeks flush pink again, and I reach out and place my hand on hers before she can hide behind her hair.

"What if I told you I don't know what I want to do?"

I shrug. "I wouldn't believe you."

Her eyebrows shoot up. "Why not?"

"You seem like the type to have your entire life planned out."

She bites her lower lip and stares at her dinner plate, lost in thought. "Maybe I used to, but I don't know anymore."

"Then tell me your former life's ambition."

There's another long pause, and a wry smile crosses her lips. She shakes her head, and says, "I wanted to be a makeup artist. Like, stage makeup."

My eyes light up. "We could totally work together."

She shakes her head. "I'm not going for that anymore."

"Oh." I can hear my disappointment dripping from that one syllable. "What are you going for then?"

She shrugs. "I have no idea."

I study her face, trying to bore into her soul and really read her. Finally, I say, "Do you still love it?"

"Of course." The answer comes automatically. No hesitation.

"Then why give it up?"

She crosses her free arm over her chest and stays quiet. She's starting to shut down on me. I give the hand I'm still holding a little squeeze and give her an out.

"You don't have to answer if you don't want," I say gently. "I mean, someday I hope you'll trust me with your secrets, but it doesn't have to be right now."

She lets out a slow breath, relief, I think.

"But I wanted to ask you one more thing. About that Rachel girl."

Her gaze darts up to mine, and she inhales a sharp breath.

"There's clearly some bad blood. Will you tell me what happened?"

She scowls and pulls her hand away, and I'm sure I've blown it. *Stupid.* Why did I have to ask her this on our first real date?

She chews her lower lip for a moment, wringing her hands on the table between us. "You won't want to hear it."

"Try me." I give her my most charming smile.

"She kissed my boyfriend. *Ex*-boyfriend," she quickly corrects herself.

I don't like to hear her say the word *boyfriend* if she's not talking about me, but I keep that thought to myself. "Oh."

She closes her eyes, drawing in a deep breath and letting it out slowly. "I was supposed to go to prom with him last year, but I got sick. I asked him to take *her* instead, because I knew she really wanted to go, and she was my best friend. But then, a few days after the dance he came to my house and told me she kissed him. I was pissed, especially when *she* came to my house later that day and told me *he* kissed *her*." Shaking her head, she finally meets my eyes. "I didn't know who to believe, so I dumped them both."

I sit in silence for a few beats, absorbing what she's just told me. Two thoughts are running through my mind. First, who in their right mind would cheat on someone as amazing as Summer? And two, how hard must it be to lose both your boyfriend and your best friend in one go?

"How long were you together?"

"Bradley and I only dated a couple months. I'm *so* over him."

That's a relief to hear. "What about your friendship with Rachel? How long were you friends?"

"Nine years."

"Ouch."

"Yep."

I try to imagine Mark or Abigail kissing Summer. I'd probably punch them, and I'm not the violent type. I can imagine the pain Summer went through, but I also don't think I could just give up on the friendship. It's a dick move, but that's a lot of years of friendship to throw away over a single kiss.

"Have you talked to her?"

"No." The word is like a dagger, aimed at Rachel, but I feel the force of it.

"Nine years is a long friendship to let go of."

"Believe me, I know."

I narrow my eyes, studying her. I can see the anger on her face, but I can also see the hurt. I hate seeing her hurting. I decide we need a topic change.

"Are you done eating?"

She looks down at her plate, and shrugs. "Yeah. I'm done."

I pay the bill and lead her down to the water's edge. "We have some time to kill before the movie, let's walk."

She lets me hold her hand, and we walk in silence for a little while, taking in the view of the ocean. This moment is perfect, walking along the oceanside with the girl of my dreams.

"You know," she begins, "before I met you, I never really did this."

"Did what?"

"Nothing." She shakes her head and gestures with her free hand. "I was always so busy, either with volleyball or my blog, show choir or debate club, or whatever. I never did just...nothing."

"This isn't nothing," I tell her. "This is walking in one of the most beautiful places on earth with the most beautiful girl in the world."

Her cheeks flush pink. Before she can hide behind her hair, I stop walking and place my hand on her cheek. She looks up at me, and I smile, then lean forward and press my lips to hers.

The kiss is brief. I'd stand there all evening kissing her if I could, but we have a movie to catch.

We head back to the car and drive to the theater. At the ticket booth I pull out a couple of bills and pay before she has a chance to unzip her purse. Grinning, I put my cast arm over her shoulder and take the tickets with my other hand.

"How long again until you get that thing off?" she asks.

"Three days." I grin proudly.

"Good, no offense, but it's looking a little rough."

I laugh and pass our tickets to the kid at the ticket stand. He hands me the stubs and directs us toward our auditorium.

"Popcorn?" I say.

"Kane. We *just* ate."

"Okay. More for me." I steer her toward the concession stand and get in line. When it's our turn, I order a large popcorn and soda combo. Turning to Summer, I ask, "Are you sure you don't want anything? Last chance."

She bites her lower lip, and I wait. After a few seconds she says, "M&M's. Plain."

I snatch a package of M&M's from the display beside us and

toss it on the counter. After paying, Summer takes pity on me and carries the popcorn and candy, while I carry the soda.

When we reach our auditorium, I let Summer pick the seats. Where someone sits in a theater says a lot about a person. Like, if she wants to sit in the way back, does that mean she wants to skip the movie and make out? I don't have to worry about whether she wants to or not, because she chooses two seats dead center. This also happens to be my favorite place to sit; to me it says, "I'm here for the movie."

We settle in for the previews. Every time a good looking one comes on, I lean over and whisper, "I have to see that one!" in her ear. Sometimes she comments back, but mostly she just smiles that tiny almost smile of hers.

About twenty minutes into the film, I realize the girl who didn't want concessions has eaten half the bag of M&M's and a good portion of my popcorn. I offer her the drink to wash the snacks down. She hesitates, then accepts. It's too dark to tell, but I'm fairly certain she's blushing.

"So, how was my popcorn?" I jest when the credits begin to roll, and the house lights come up.

"I'm so sorry," she says, hiding her face behind her hands. "I really wasn't hungry, but if you put popcorn in front of me, I *will* eat it. I probably should have warned you."

I laugh and wrap an arm around her shoulder, squeezing her close to my side. "It's okay. I really don't mind."

"Are you sure?" she asks. "I should probably pay you for half."

"Don't be crazy. This date is my treat."

She reaches into the popcorn tub and is met with the nasty, crumbly kernels at the bottom.

"Come on, we'll grab a refill before we go."

"No popcorn allowed in my mom's car, sorry."

"We'll eat it in the parking lot then, outside the car."

"Deal."

I eat slowly, ignoring my mom's curfew, and try to make this date last as long as possible. But as they say, all good things must come to an end. All too soon, our popcorn tub is in the trash outside the theater entrance, and she's driving me home. I don't want to say goodbye to Summer. She's finally starting to let me see behind her walls.

"So, on a scale of one to ten, how would you rate this date?" I ask, as Summer pulls into my driveway and puts the car in park.

"What?" she asks in surprise.

"You heard me." I grin, waiting for her answer.

"Is ten good or bad?"

"Ten is awesome."

"Hmm..." She pauses for a long moment, appearing to really consider things. "An eight."

I scoff. "An *eight*? Really? I bring you to one of the *best* restaurants in Southern California and you give me an *eight*?"

She purses her lips and studies my face. Her gaze lingers on my lips for a moment, and her cheeks grow pink. "There's still time to make it a ten..."

She ducks her head toward the steering wheel. Her hair falls forward and conceals her face.

I grin and lean across the center console. I push her hair behind her ear with my left hand and she tilts her face up toward me. I close the distance and press my lips to hers.

Her arm snakes around my neck, and I take that as my cue to tangle my fingers in her hair. For a half second, I wonder if she uses special shampoo or if her hair is naturally that soft. The thought is gone as quickly as it came. I'm too focused again on her lips and their every tiny movement against mine.

I could kiss Summer all day every day, and it still wouldn't be enough. All too soon, she pulls back. I reluctantly release her, slowly running my fingers through her hair as I disentangle them. I'm delighted to see her cheeks are even more flushed now. She gives me a shy smile and runs a hand through her hair, fixing the mess I've made.

"So, ten?" I ask hopefully.

Her eyes meet mine, and if I think her cheeks can't get any pinker, I'm wrong. She tries to hide her smile, and says, "Eleven."

I pump my fist before I can stop myself, muttering, "Yes!"

A quiet laugh comes from Summer beside me. I look over and grin shamelessly.

"What are you doing tomorrow? There's a cool event going on and I want to take you."

She hesitates, her lower lip pulled between her teeth again. I wait, holding my breath as I count the seconds until she replies.

"Sure."

"Can I pick you up on my bike, or will you want to drive?"

She chuckles. "How far are we going?"

"Not far."

She narrows her eyes, then says, "Okay. You can drive."

I grin. "You won't be disappointed. Eleven sharp. Be ready." I lean across the seat and give her one last lingering kiss. "Sweet dreams."

I exit the car and race to my house, turning to wave when I reach the door. She backs out of my driveway and takes off down my street. I wait until the vehicle is out of sight before entering my house.

"How was your big date?" Mom calls from the living room.

I follow her voice and collapse on the couch beside her. "Mom, that's the girl I'm going to marry."

18

SUMMER

I finish slathering my skin with sunscreen and stare out my front window, waiting for Kane. I can't believe I'm going on another date with him. What happened to my resolve? I'm so selfish. I shouldn't let him fall for me, not when I'm so broken. But I'm afraid it's too late anyway. He's already in too deep.

At promptly 11 AM, I see him tearing down the road on his bike. I sling my purse over my shoulder and yell, "I'm going out with a friend. Bye!"

I bolt out the door and meet him at the end of my driveway.

"I know, I break you and you'll kill me," he greets me with that big, adorable, goofy grin of his.

I smile at him then glance at my house. "You know it. Now let's go." I hop onto my usual spot on his handlebars. This is becoming *way* too normal.

"What's the big rush?"

I twist my upper body and look him in the eye. "I don't want to have the whole meet the parents drama right now."

He frowns, and I turn to face forward again. I can't remember ever seeing him without a smile. Even when he was sitting in the urgent care with a broken bone and bloody chin, he still had a grin on his face. I hope I didn't hurt his feelings. I'm just not that open with my parents. They never even met Bradley, and we dated for three months.

Kane pedals away from my house in silence. We ride like that until we reach the beach.

I hop off the handlebars. "Do you ever go anywhere besides the boardwalk, the skatepark, and urgent care?"

"Sure. School."

I look at him skeptically. I actually don't mind being here again, but I *am* wondering what's so amazing that he had to bring me here *today*. I won't admit it to anyone but going out two days in a row is really draining me.

"Trust me, you're going to love this." He flashes me his trademark grin then chains his bike to the rack. He slings an arm over my shoulder and guides me down the boardwalk toward the parking lot. The place is extra busy, even for a Saturday.

"What is going on today?" I ask, scanning the busy area in bewilderment.

Kane is practically bouncing with excitement. "Food trucks!"

"What?" I ask in surprise.

"A whole bunch of food trucks are here today. I can't wait to buy you my favorites."

I stand still as a statue for a moment and take in the scene. An area of the parking lot is sectioned off and there are food trucks lined up, each decorated in bright colors. Pictures of food and the menus decorate the sides. Crowds of people are milling around, many with containers of food from the trucks.

Kane gives my arm a light squeeze and guides me into the chaos. I try to disguise my reaction. I wasn't sure what to expect from today, but it wasn't this. And I sort of love this.

"Have you ever had Ming's Egg Rolls?" He points to a food truck painted in reds and yellows and covered in Chinese characters.

I shake my head, still trying to take in everything.

"What about Paco's Tacos?"

I shake my head again. "I've never actually eaten from a food truck," I admit. "Except for ice cream."

Kane freezes in place, then turns to gape at me. He removes his arm from around me and places both his hands on my shoulders. He stares into my eyes, and a tingle of warmth spreads through my body at his touch.

"You poor sheltered soul." His voice is as serious as his face. "You don't even know how lucky you are to have me."

I smile. "Thank goodness for urgent care then."

He nods once, the motion definitive. "Exactly. It was fate. I've been sent to show you the wonder of food trucks."

"Lead the way, *Oh Wise One*."

He releases my shoulders and grabs my hand again, leading me through the crowd of food truck patrons.

Our first stop is Paco's Tacos, where he orders only enough food for one. I grab the food while he pays. It smells amazing.

He winks, then leads me to the next truck. "We're getting something from every truck," he explains.

I look warily at the taco in his hand. I really shouldn't be sharing food with anyone, not with my lupus. But how is this any different from kissing him? Or downing half his soda at the movie last night? I smile and take a bite of the taco before offering it to him. He leans forward and takes a massive bite, spilling taco guts all over the pavement and the front of his shirt. I laugh.

"Oh crap." He brushes the lettuce and ground beef off his shirt. It's another food pun shirt. This one says, "All I wanna do is eat tacos with you (or without you, I'm here for the tacos.)"

By the time we're done, we've sampled one food item from seven different food trucks.

"So, what was your favorite?" he asks, taking a bite of a gyro before offering the last of it to me.

"You're putting me on the spot," I answer, letting him pop the last bite directly into my mouth. I chew and think, then say, "It might have to be Paco's Tacos."

Kane pumps his fist, then holds his hand up for a high five. "Excellent answer," he says when I slap his hand.

We finish with the last of our food truck fare, then he leads me down the boardwalk.

"Time to burn off all those calories?" I ask jokingly.

"Didn't I tell you? Food truck calories don't count."

"Ri-ight," I reply, drawing out the word.

He slips his hand in mine. "Actually, I just didn't want to take you home yet. I like spending time with you."

"I... like spending time with you too," I admit. I glance at him from the corner of my eye. He's grinning ear to ear. I have another moment of panic, hoping I'm not setting us both up for heartache and disappointment.

19

KANE

I'm finally going to do it," Abigail announces, setting her lunch tray down at our usual table.

"Do what?" Summer asks, looking between Abigail, Mark, and me.

"I'm getting a tattoo." Abigail is grinning ear to ear, a mischievous twinkle in her eye.

"Uh huh," Mark says from his place beside her. He pops a tortilla chip into his mouth.

"You don't believe me," Abigail accuses.

"It's just that..." I begin. "How can I put this delicately?"

Mark snorts, and I shoot him a glare. He speaks up before I can finish. "You always *say* you're going to get a tattoo, Abz, but you never follow through."

Abigail elbows him in the ribs. It's refreshing to see someone else on that end of her annoyance for once. "This time I'm serious. I'm going sometime this week, after school."

"What are you getting?" Summer asks. When I turn to face her, she looks genuinely curious.

"A seahorse."

"Cute. Where?"

I hadn't pegged Summer as the kind of girl to get a tattoo. Her level of interest in Abigail's has me second guessing though.

"I'm not sure yet."

"Well, where are you considering?"

Summer leans forward in her seat, bringing herself closer to Abigail. A bubble of jealousy creeps forward, and I push it back. I know Summer wants to be with me and not Abigail. Our weekend together is proof enough of that. She rated our first real date an *eleven* after all. But still, even though I want her to get along with my friends, it's hard to share her.

"You should come with me," Abigail says, a mischievous twinkle in her eye. I look between the girls. While I've been fending off the green monster, I've missed part of their conversation.

"Okay, but only if you'll go dress shopping with me for homecoming."

"Deal," Abigail agrees. "I suppose I'll need a dress too." She shoots me a glare, and I smile in return.

"Don't you have to be eighteen to get a tattoo?" Mark asks, changing the subject.

"I know a guy," Abigail says with a sly smile.

"Won't your parents kill you?" Summer asks. Her excitement over their pending excursion seems to fade as the age limitation sinks in.

Abigail shrugs. "I'll get it somewhere they won't see it."

"What's the point in a tattoo nobody can see?" I ask, baffled. I have no plans for getting a tattoo, but if I did, I'd get a whole sleeve and wear it proudly.

"*I'll* know I have it," Abigail states, giving me a look that shows what she thinks of my intelligence.

"Fair enough," I relent.

Abigail turns her attention back to Summer. "So, when are we doing this?"

"Meet you by the flagpole after school tomorrow?"

"Deal."

Mom is waiting for me in her car when I arrive home after school.

"Come on, Kane! Let's not be late."

I let my bike fall into the grass at the side of the driveway, even though Mom hates when I do that. I jog to the car, toss my backpack on the backseat, and then climb into the passenger side.

My cast is finally coming off today. As soon as Dr. Roberts releases me, I'm grabbing my board and heading to the skatepark.

When Mom parks, I'm out of the car before she is.

"Come on, Mom. Let's not be late!" I throw her words back at her, then race for the building. I push the door open, and I'm greeted by the twenty-something receptionist.

"Hey, Missy, how's it going?" I ask, leaning against the counter and grinning.

"I'm well, how are you, Kane?" Her gaze lands on my cast. "Is that thing finally coming off?"

"Yep."

Mom enters, and Missy hands over the paperwork for her to sign. She takes a seat in the waiting area, while I stay and chat with Missy.

We don't have to wait long before the nurse, Nora, calls me back.

"Dr. Roberts will be in soon to get that cast off," she tells us, once we're settled in the room, and leaves.

Mom smiles at me. "Did you learn anything from this experience?"

I shrug. "Don't land on my wrist when I fall?"

She shakes her head. "How about, keep both feet on the ground?"

"Mom. That's *so* boring."

There's a short rap on the exam room door, and then it opens. Dr. Roberts appears in the doorway, carrying a laptop and a tray with a cast saw and other medical supplies.

"Kane, how's that wrist feeling?"

"Amazing, Dr. R. I'm ready for this thing to come off."

He smiles and picks up a marker. "Then let's do this."

After marking a line on both sides of the cast, he picks up the saw, then makes an incision on both the top and bottom. A few snips with the scissors and the cast is off.

"Oh, god," Mom says, covering her mouth and nose with her hand. "I'd forgotten about the smell."

Dr. Roberts chuckles. "Take it easy, Kane. Your wrist is going to be weak for a while. I've got some exercises for you to work on to build your strength back up."

"I remember from the last time," I tell him. I eye the cast sitting on the table. "Can I keep that?"

"No!" Mom exclaims.

"But, Mom," I object. "Summer signed it."

Mom gives me *The Look*. "You can have her sign a piece of paper. That smelly thing is not coming back into my house."

I sigh and stare forlornly at the cast. Before I needed that cast, Summer didn't know I was alive. Maybe Mom's right, though. I don't need the smelly old cast with her signature, not when I can kiss the girl pretty much whenever I want.

Before we leave Dr. Robert's office, Mom forces me to scrub the hell out of my wrist for the same reason she refused to let me keep the cast. I suppose the strong scent of antiseptic soap is an upgrade from the cast smell.

I forget all about that when we arrive home and mom reluctantly returns my skateboard.

"Do *not*," she says, "I repeat, *do not*, make me regret this."

I give her my most angelic smile and promise. My appointment took up enough of the afternoon that there isn't time to make a real dinner, so we have sandwiches. Mom excuses herself to work in her office, and I grab my board and tell her I'm heading out.

Though I can't travel as fast on my board as I can on my bike, it's nice to have it back. I do a few simple ollies in the driveway to get the feel of my board again, then take off for the skatepark.

"Look who got his cast off," Dennis says, as I skate up to the arch. "How's it feel?"

I grin. "It feels good. I can't wait to get back to it."

"Right on, man." He looks around, as though he's expecting someone. "What happened to that cute chick? You haven't brought her around again."

I narrow my eyes at him. "Summer?"

"Yeah. That sounds right."

I shrug. "Skating's not really her thing."

Annoyed with Dennis, I skate into the park and text Mark and Abigail. I tell them the good news; I'm cast free and back at it.

I spend the next twenty minutes skating around the park, testing out the simpler tricks I know. I promised Mom I wouldn't break anything today, so I play it safe. Finally, I see Mark and Abigail walking under the arch from the parking lot. I skate over to the entrance to greet them.

"Wow, that's so gross," Abigail says, her gaze fixed on my wrist and lips curled in disgust. I glance down and shrug. My skin is pale and peeling. The foul odor clings to my skin, though not as strong as it was on the cast itself.

"It's only been free for like, an hour," I tell her. "It'll be better tomorrow."

"I hope so, because I don't want to eat lunch with that thing nearby."

20

SUMMER

I'm a little anxious today. School itself was fine, and I actually slept well last night, which is good, but today I have plans with Abigail. As promised, she meets me after school to go dress shopping. Mark was planning to surf anyway, so he drove us to the boardwalk, and from there we walked to a row of boutiques in search of formal wear for Homecoming.

"I hate everything," Abigail declares, holding up a green beaded formal dress. She glares at it in disgust.

"That dress isn't *that* awful," I say.

"Sure, if you look good in booger green."

I laugh. "Okay, but aside from the *color*, it's not that bad."

Abigail scrunches her nose and shoves the offending dress back on the rack.

I pull a yellow strapless dress from the rack, and immediately return it. The dress selection isn't awesome, but it's also not as bad as Abigail is making it out to be.

"Are you looking forward to the dance?" I get the feeling she's not really into school dances and wonder why she's even going.

"I don't know, it might be fun," she says, eyeing a black satin number. "School dances aren't usually my thing, but..." She shrugs. "What about you?"

I turn away from her and feign interest in another booger-green dress—seriously, who decided this color was *in* this season? I keep my back to Abigail. If she sees my face right now, she'll see that I'm not entirely sure about going to homecoming. School dances were supposed to be a part of the old life I gave up, but somehow Kane has pulled me back.

"Sure," I finally say, when I'm sure my voice is steady. "What's not to look forward to?"

"The awful music. The B.O. The overly sweet punch. Need I go on?"

I laugh and turn back to her. My gaze lands on the dress she's still holding. It's simple, but elegant. "You need to try that on."

"You think?" She looks at the dress again. "I suppose it's not awful." A devious grin appears on her lips, and she meets my eye. "I'll try it on, but only if you try on the booger green one."

I laugh. "No way! If I'm going to try on that hideous dress, you need to try it on, too."

"Deal."

We both hasten our search of the racks, picking out the ugliest dresses we can find for the other to try on. I pause when I come across a whimsical pale blue number in my size, then add it to the pile. When our arms are full, we find the fitting rooms and try on the ugliest dresses first, modeling for one another. I can't remember the last time I laughed so hard.

"Wait, we need to capture this moment," I tell Abigail, when we both step out of our respective rooms wearing the booger-green dresses. I grab my phone from my purse hanging on the door and we pose in front of the mirror while I snap photos.

We lean over the screen and inspect the images. Abigail breaks into laughter. When she finally recovers, she says, "You should send that to Kane and tell him that's what you're wearing."

"No way! What if he buys me a snot corsage?"

Abigail loses it again, and we retreat to our respective rooms to try on our next dresses. I realize I'm out of ugly dresses, and I'm left facing the blue one hanging all by its lonesome on the wall hook. I slip it on and stare at my reflection in the mirror. It's perfect. The fabric is a silky, baby blue satin with a sweetheart neckline and a mermaid cut. From the top down past my hips, the material is ruched and studded with scattered rhinestones. From there, it cascades to the floor in soft billowy layers. It reminds me of the ocean waves rippling toward shore. It fits me like a glove, and I hope my medication doesn't cause me to gain any weight, because this is the dress I'm wearing to the dance.

I step out of the room and knock on Abigail's door across the aisle. "Are you dressed yet?"

Abigail opens the door and my mouth falls open when I see her. The black dress clings to her curves, and the contrast with her red hair is striking. The only embellishment on the dress is a row of ruby beads along the sweetheart neckline.

"What?"

I shake my head and find my words again. "You look amazing."

Abigail smirks, then, rolling her eyes, says, "You're still not my type."

I grin. "Buy that dress. You were *born* to wear that dress."

"You really think so?" She turns this way and that in front of the mirror. The corners of her lips turn up in a smile. "I guess it's not bad."

"Now we need shoes."

Abigail groans, abandoning the mirror and returning to her fitting room. "You're buying that blue dress," she calls through the door.

Grinning, I return to my own room. I look at my reflection once more, pulling my hair up to better envision my Homecoming look. I drop my hair and reluctantly pull off the dress.

Once back in our own clothes, Abigail and I hang our rejected dresses on the return rack and venture to the wall of shoes. Abigail chooses a pair of black strappy sandals. I shake my head and take them from her. After checking the size, I place them back on the shelf and grab a nearly identical pair in red. She cocks an eyebrow at me, then tries them on, holding the dress in front of her.

"Done," I say, crossing my arms over my chest to solidify the finality of my statement.

"I do like the red. Your turn." Abigail throws the shoes back in the box, tucks it under her arm, and turns back to the shoe selection.

"Oooh," she squeals. Her back is to me, and her body is blocking whatever she's found. Turning, she shows off a pump in the horrid snot green color.

A snort escapes my lips and we both fall into a round of laughter.

"It's fate. Put back the blue dress and go grab the green."

"Not if it was the last dress on earth," I say, struggling to breathe through my laughter.

Abigail puts the shoe back, and once I've recovered, she holds up a pair of simple silver glittery sandals. "These?"

"Yes," I say, taking the shoe from her. It's not my size, but I find my size and try them on. Holding the dress in front of me, I stand in front of the mirror and scrutinize my appearance. "These are perfect."

We stop by the accessories department and find a cute black and red clutch for Abigail. I have a silver one at home, so I don't buy one for myself. After a stop at a nearby jewelry boutique we're set.

We exit the shop and step into the sunny afternoon. I slip my sunglasses on, and I follow Abigail's lead.

"Want to come over the day of the dance and do hair and makeup together?" I've been working up the courage to ask her this all day. It'll be weird getting ready for a school dance without Rachel, but maybe it'll be less weird if Abigail takes her place?

"Sure," Abigail agrees. "But only if you get a tattoo with me."

I freeze in place. Get a tattoo? Sure, I've always wanted one. But right now? *Today?* My parents would absolutely *kill me* if they found out. I bite my lip and try to slow my racing heart.

Abigail realizes I've stopped moving and pauses. Looking over her shoulder, she scrutinizes my reaction, and says, "Kidding." Her own sunglasses shield her eyes, but she's grinning. "I'll get ready with you whether you get a tattoo or not."

I breathe a sigh of relief and adjust the shopping bags on my arm. "So, where are we heading next?"

"My brother has a friend who is training to be a tattoo artist. He's doing them super cheap. His apartment is in walking distance."

My jaw drops and my eyebrows shoot up. "Wait, you're getting a tattoo from some guy in his *apartment?* Doesn't this sound a little dangerous to you?"

Abigail shrugs. "He's my brother's friend. I've met him before, it'll be fine." Her voice is both casual and confident. Clearly, she sees nothing sketchy about this situation.

Reluctantly, I follow. Though I'm still not sold on this being a good idea, I'd rather stay with her. Safety in numbers and all that. We walk a few blocks, make a few turns away from the coast, and stop in front of a sketchy looking apartment building.

Abigail presses a buzzer and a voice through the speaker says, "Yeah?"

"Yo, it's Abz. Let me up."

The door buzzes and Abigail yanks it open, holding it for me to enter first. I slowly step through the doorway and enter a dimly lit hallway. It smells like sweat and stale smoke. And Abigail was complaining about the impending smell of B.O. at the dance?

"Third floor," she says, leading me to a stairwell at the end of the hall. I keep my shopping bag and purse clutched tightly to my side. I can imagine the types of unsavory characters who probably reside in this building. I also note that it doesn't have an elevator.

We take the stairwell—which smells worse than the first floor hallway did—up to the third floor. Abigail pounds on the door of number 302. We hear footsteps inside, then the door swings open.

I expected to be greeted by a large man in his thirties or forties, covered in tattoos and wearing a beater. Probably with a full beard and a cigarette hanging out of his mouth. So I'm surprised by the man who opens the door. He can't be older than his mid-twenties. He's Hispanic and wearing a gray t-shirt. He sports no facial hair, and I can see a single tattoo on his bicep. My anxiety level instantly decreases.

"Come on in," he says, smiling at Abigail. His gaze lands on me and he eyes me curiously. "Who's your friend, Abz?"

He holds the door open and Abigail enters. I follow close behind, taking in the apartment decor. It's clearly a bachelor pad, but not dirty. There's a brown sofa in the corner and a large screen TV with a jumble of video games and controllers on the floor. Not much different than I'd expect to see in any guy's house. The kitchen is off to my right. Aside from a few dirty dishes I can see poking up from the sink, it's fairly clean and ordinary. My anxiety is almost completely gone now.

"This is Summer. She's a friend from school." Turning to me, Abigail says, "This is Aaron Mendez. He went to school with my brother, Jared."

"Nice to meet you, Summer. You here for a tattoo as well?"

"Uh..."

Abigail laughs. "She's just here to watch."

"Let me know if you change your mind." He turns his attention back to Abigail. "So, you know what you want?"

"Yep. But let me take a peek through your book again anyway."

Aaron pulls out a binder and sets it on the kitchen table.

Abigail takes a seat and flips through pages of tattoo designs. I look over her shoulder. "Did you do all of these?" I ask.

"Yep. See anything that catches your eye?"

The designs are good. When Abigail said he was training to be a tattoo artist, I'd assumed he'd suck. Quite a few of the designs catch my eye, but my attention lingers on a dragonfly on the current page.

"This is the one," Abigail says, stabbing her finger in the book and pointing at a seahorse on the same page as my dragonfly.

"Cool." Aaron reaches out to take the book from her.

"Can I look through that?" I say quickly. I'm fascinated by the artwork in the book.

Aaron cocks an eyebrow, then hands the book to me. I take a seat in the chair next to Abigail, while Aaron prepares the materials for the tattoo. His portfolio contains a diverse variety of tattoos. There are skulls and dragons, but also more dainty designs like the dragonfly, seahorse, and flowers. I keep coming back to the dragonfly.

Abigail sucks in a breath, catching my attention. I realize Aaron has started, and I watch as the tattoo machine traces a line across the flesh of Abigail's hip. Blood bubbles up and Aaron wipes it away with a cloth, then continues with the design. The buzz of the tattoo machine is almost hypnotic. When he finishes, Abigail's skin beneath the black ink is red, but the tattoo looks awesome.

"This is so cool," Abigail says, twisting her torso to admire her new ink. Aaron hands her a hand mirror and she stands, adjusting the mirror to get a better look.

"Change your mind?" Aaron asks. His smile is warm and inviting, and I think, *what the hell?*

Pointing to the dragonfly on the open page, I say, "How much for this one?"

Before I know it, I'm sitting in Abigail's vacated seat with my bare hip exposed, waiting for the needle to begin injecting ink into my skin.

"You're braver than I thought, Swanson," Abigail says. She's standing nearby, admiring the little seahorse on her hip.

I'm too nervous to speak, so I smile instead. I can't believe I'm doing this. I take a deep breath and try to relax. My parents would kill me if they knew. My doctors would probably lecture me too. But I've been feeling great and haven't had a flare up in weeks. I'll be fine. It's just a tattoo. I'd researched on my phone during class after Abigail mentioned her tattoo at lunch. People with Lupus get tattoos all the time.

I flinch when the needle presses into my skin, but I clench my teeth and try to think happy thoughts. Like my new Homecoming dress. And how I felt when Kane was kissing me. It helps.

When he's done, Aaron plucks the hand mirror from Abigail's hands and places it in mine. I angle it so I can see my tattoo clearly. It's adorable, a black outline of a delicate dragonfly. It's large enough to show detail in the wings, but small enough that I should be able to hide it under all my clothes. Including my bathing suits, if I ever go swimming again.

"That is *so* cute," Abigail gushes, turning her attention from her tattoo and focusing on mine. "I would totally get that if I didn't already have an entire ocean theme planned for my body."

"Wait, *what*?" My eyebrows shoot up in surprise.

Abigail nods proudly. "Yep. My body is my canvas and I plan to display my love for all sea life on it."

I shake my head. "I think I'm done." I study her seahorse for a moment, Abigail's pale skin is still red and raised beneath the black ink. I'd be worried, but I read that this was normal. I glance at my own dragonfly and notice my skin is reacting the same way.

Aaron takes the mirror from my hand and covers my tattoo with gauze. I'm sad to see it hidden, but I know it's for the best.

"What's next?" I ask Abigail. Gesturing to her body, I elaborate. "For your tattoos."

"I don't know what I'll get next, but I know I want to get some scales, maybe behind my ear. I also want a shark somewhere, either a hammerhead or a great white, I haven't decided. I'll probably get a turtle, maybe on my foot?" She looks contemplative for a moment and I can tell she's put a lot of thought into this. "I also saw a really cool mermaid tat online that went all the way down the girl's side, from the top of her ribs to her hips. I need that. Maybe that will be my college graduation gift to myself."

I shake my head. "Wow." Abigail is so much braver than I am.

Aaron finishes covering my tattoo, and I snap the closure on my jean shorts. I wait for Abigail to have her bandage applied. We hand over our cash and Aaron walks us to the door, inviting us back any time for more tattoos. The stench in the hall doesn't seem as bad on the way out, but I'm still grateful when we step outside and I'm able to take in a big whiff of fresh air. Well, as fresh as the air in Southern California ever is.

"Want to grab some grub?" Abigail asks.

I shrug. "Sure. I guess I could eat."

I fall into step beside her, as she sets off in the direction of the boardwalk. She continues telling me about her big tattoo plans, pointing out places on her body she wants to ink. It's nice to have a friend again. Until Kane pulled me into his orbit, I hadn't realized just how lonely I'd been.

A sudden pang of guilt floods through me. It's not fair for me to make friends with Abigail and Kane. They're nice people who don't deserve to have to deal with someone as broken as me. It's been weeks since my last flare up, which means I'm probably due for one any day now. And then what? I'll probably be out sick from school, and all my new friends will figure out how broken I am. They'll regret ever having wasted time on me. And it'll be my fault.

"Hey, are you okay?" Abigail asks, pausing mid-stride and looking at me in concern.

I shake my head and lower myself to the curb. "I think I need to sit down for a moment." We're almost to the boardwalk. I can see the beach at the end of the street, mocking me.

"You look pale." Abigail chews on a fingernail as she studies my face.

"I'm fine. Sorry." I quickly try to make up an excuse for my behavior that isn't incredibly lame. "I think the excitement of the tattoo just caught up to me."

Abigail takes a seat beside me. "I get it."

"You do?" I look at her in surprise.

"Sure. You're probably thinking of all the ways your parents will murder you if they find out."

That *wasn't* what I was thinking, but I am *now*.

"You're a little more badass than I thought," Abigail adds.

"So, am I your type now?" I try to joke, but it sounds hollow to my ears.

Abigail laughs and slings an arm around my shoulders. "Not even close, Marcia."

I narrow my eyes. "Marcia?"

"You're a regular Marcia Brady. A goody two-shoes."

I roll my eyes. I'm feeling better, so I push myself to standing. "Come on, let's get that grub."

21

KANE

I still can't believe Summer is mine. We haven't put a label on us, I was too afraid of scaring her off before, but I think it's time. I mean, she clearly likes spending time with me. She eats lunch at my table more often than not, and she agreed to be my Homecoming date. Plus, she seems to like kissing me. All signs point to her saying yes to *officially* being my girlfriend when I ask.

Tonight.

Some kids from school are throwing a party at the beach. She hesitated when I asked her to come, but she said yes. She picks me up from my house, and when we arrive, we walk hand in hand to the large fire burning in the sand.

We stop by the flames to say hi to Abigail, Mark, and other people we know. The fire pops and cracks, and lavender flames spout forth as a guy from school tosses a driftwood log on the flame.

A whooping cheer erupts from David Aster and a group of his friends. The small brunette with them glares at the guys.

David catches her look, rolls his eyes, and says, "Lighten up, Hannah."

"Uh oh," I mutter, pulling my gaze from the scene and looking around.

"What?" Summer asks.

But I don't need to answer.

Abigail strides across the sand—fuming—and grabs the kid who threw the log in the fire by the ear. "What the hell, Andrew?"

I glance at Summer. Her eyes are wide with surprise, as Abigail drags the kid away from the fire, reading him the riot act the whole time.

"Don't you know that burning driftwood releases toxins into the air," Abigail demands. "Not to mention the animals that rely on that wood for shelter."

"Whoa," Summer whispers, as Abigail drags the kid out of earshot.

"Abigail can be..." I search for the right word. "Intense."

"You don't say?"

I laugh. "Come on." I gently tug her by the hand, leading her down to the water's edge.

"What are we doing?" she asks. My fingers intertwine with hers as we walk along the shore.

"Well, I'm a Sagittarius and enjoy long walks on the beach..."

Laughing, Summer playfully rams her shoulder into my arm, but keeps pace.

"Sorry." I laugh. "I just wanted to be alone with you for a little while."

"Okay." The wind blows a strand of hair into her face, and she tucks it behind her ear.

"I really like spending time with you, Summer."

She ducks her head, her long locks falling forward and shielding her from my view. She does this a lot, especially when I say things like this to her. I wonder if she even realizes she's doing it.

"And," I continue, "I wanted to ask you something."

She comes out of hiding and looks me in the eye now. "Yeah?"

"You're supposed to say that after I ask you." It's a dumb joke, but I can't resist.

She rolls her eyes, but she's smiling, so I consider it a win.

"I'd like you to be my girlfriend," I tell her.

"That's not a question," she says softly, staring out at the waves.

My turn to roll my eyes. I take a deep breath, then rephrase my statement as a question, "*Will* you be my girlfriend, Summer?"

Summer stops walking and turns to face me, pulling her hand from my grasp. I curl my hands into fists, missing the feel of hers, then release them. She doesn't say anything for a very long moment, and I brace myself for her rejection.

She studies me, her eyes searching my face, then she reaches up and wraps her arms around my neck. I grin and tilt my head forward, allowing her to press her lips to mine.

We're interrupted by the sound of catcalls coming from somewhere behind us. I want to ignore them and lose myself in the feel of her soft lips, but she releases me. Her cheeks flush pink in the fading light, and she hides behind her hair again.

Grinning like an idiot, I take her hand in mine. "So...is that a yes?"

"Yes."

Releasing her hand, I wrap my arm around her shoulders and pull her close to my side. As we walk, the sound of music, laughter, and the crackling fire grow fainter as we distance ourselves from the party.

As dusk falls, and the pinks and purples in the sky gradually give way to black, Summer and I make our way across the sand and back toward the blazing fire. The breeze coming off the ocean is cold now that we're no longer cooking under the fading rays of the sun.

Our classmates are grouped around the flames in small clusters of friends. Summer sits beside me in the sand near the fire. Despite wearing a long-sleeved t-shirt, she's shivering, her hands tucked into her sleeves. I wrap my arm around her, hoping my body heat and the fire are enough to warm her, and cursing myself for not bringing a hoodie for her.

Summer relaxes against me and releases a long breath. Score one point for Kane, I'm on my way to becoming boyfriend of the year.

Nearby, someone is telling ghost stories, but there's more laughter than shrieks of fear. I'm too hyper focused on Summer's close proximity to pay anyone else much attention. Her familiar coconut scent has me captive, it's light and sweet and reminds me of the beach.

I glance around and take a mental picture. Someday, I can tell my grandkids all about the night Summer said yes to being my girlfriend.

David, the guy who was cheering over the driftwood flames earlier, is blasting music from a bluetooth speaker. His arm is slung around Hannah, but his attention is on a group of guys nearby. Behind them, some other guys and a few girls are playing frisbee. I wonder how that's going, considering how dark it is now.

Halfway around the fire, I spy Abigail seated beside Mark. She grins and gives me a thumbs up. Mark's focus is on something across the fire. He's probably wishing he was riding the waves right now, even though that would be stupid dangerous with the lack of visibility and increased chance of shark attack.

My attention returns to Summer, and I smile. She feels good snuggled against my side, under my arm. I could get used to this.

After a little while, Abigail approaches, flopping into the sand beside Summer.

"How's it going, girlfriend?"

I ignore her. I'm too content right now to be annoyed with her.

Summer shrugs.

"How's your tattoo?" Abigail asks.

"Wait, *what?*" I demand, swiveling my attention to the girl leaning against me. "You got a tattoo?"

Summer shrugs. "Yeah." She turns her attention to Abigail. "It's still red and puffy."

"Mine too," Abigail says. "I'm pretty sure that's normal. It's only been a few days."

"Where is this tattoo?" I demand. "Why haven't I seen it yet?"

Abigail glares at me. "She'll show you when she's ready. It's in a fairly intimate place."

My eyes widen, and my brain starts spinning, imagining all the "intimate" places her tattoo could be. "How intimate a place?"

"It's on my hip, Kane," Summer says. "Relax."

My gaze drops to her denim clad hips.

"Stop trying to undress her with your eyes." My gaze returns to Abigail, just in time to catch her rolling her eyes.

"I'll show you eventually," Summer promises. "Once it's healed."

"Will you at least tell me what design you got?"

Summer smiles sweetly and flutters her eyelashes. "Nope."

Abigail laughs.

Ugh. These girls will be the death of me.

"Wanna ditch her—" I jerk my head toward Abigail "—and get out of here?"

Summer shrugs. "Sure. I am getting tired."

We stand and say goodbye to Abigail. I call Mark's name. He doesn't hear me, so I yell louder. His head swivels, and his eyes narrow at me in question. I grin and wave. Mark raises a hand in farewell, and Summer and I walk to the parking lot. She's still shivering, so I keep my arm around her shoulders. Next time, I'll remember a jacket or a sweater for her.

"I guess it's a good thing you drove," I tell her as we approach her mom's SUV. "You'd probably freeze on the handlebars of my bike."

She shrugs. "I'm sure I'd survive." She unlocks the doors with the keyfob, and we climb in. "But I'm glad I drove too." She hesitates a moment. Her lower lip slips between her teeth and a crease forms in her brow. "You know, you could always stay with your friends."

I shake my head. "Don't be ridiculous. I see our friends plenty. I don't get nearly enough alone time with you."

Despite the dark, semi-lit parking lot, I can just make out the adorable blush on her cheeks.

She turns the key in the ignition and pulls out of the lot and into traffic. I lean back to study her. Away from the lights in the parking lot, it's no longer semi-dark. It's just dark. I can barely make out her profile. Her focus is on the road, as she navigates the turns toward my house.

"Why are you staring at me?" She breaks the comfortable silence we'd been sitting in.

"Can't I look at you?"

She pauses. "I guess." One hand comes up and brushes her hair behind her ear, and the lip slips back between her teeth. I think I'm making her nervous.

"Did you have fun tonight?" I ask.

"Sure," she says. "It's been a while since I've been to a party."

"I don't think I've ever seen you at one of the beach bonfire parties." I *know* I haven't seen her at one, I'd have remembered.

One shoulder goes up in a shrug. "My old friends had a lot of house parties. If we had bonfires they were on private beaches by their houses, not here."

That makes sense. I remember some of her friends from the volleyball team were pretty well off and had beachfront properties. I wonder which beach party Summer prefers, but I'm afraid to ask. It's no secret that her past is a touchy subject.

She arrives at my house and parks in my driveway.

"Thanks for the lift, Girlfriend." I unfasten my seatbelt and swivel in my seat to face her.

"No problem..." She hesitates. "Boyfriend."

I grin. "I like the sound of that."

Before she can say anything, I lean forward and kiss her lips. The kiss lasts until the front lights turn on. Mom knows we're out here. I pull back and smile at her. "Goodnight."

22

SUMMER

I slip into the house and shut the door behind me as softly as I can. Locking it, I tiptoe to the stairs. I need to shut myself in my bedroom and process what I've gotten myself into.

Kane is officially my boyfriend now. It isn't lost on me that he called Abigail and Mark *our* friends. Somehow, despite my determination to remain solitary, I've become a part of their world.

A small smile creeps onto my lips, and I try to suppress it, lest someone sees and asks what I'm so happy about.

"Come here, Summer," Dad's voice rings out from the den.

I guess I wasn't as quiet as I thought. So much for sequestering myself in solitude.

Rounding the corner, I cut through the kitchen and poke my head into the den. Dad is sitting in his recliner with a newspaper in his hands. The TV is on and the screen displays a news anchor with the CNN news ticker running at the bottom, but the volume is muted. "What's up, Dad?"

"Sit down."

I really just want to go to my room and try to sleep, but it's easier to go through the motions than to argue, so I enter the den and perch on the edge of the couch across from him.

I raise my eyebrows and stare at him. I'm sure my body language tells him I'm not in the mood.

"How was your evening?"

"Um...good?"

"That's good. What were you up to?" Dad's voice is pleasant and conversational, the opposite of his courtroom voice.

I narrow my eyes, trying to get a read on the situation. Am I in trouble? Dad doesn't usually ask what I've been up to. That's always been Mom's territory. "Uh, I went to a bonfire on the beach with some friends."

"Which friends?"

"New ones. You haven't met them."

Dad sighs. "Do these new friends have names, Summer?"

I close my eyes for a moment to stop myself from rolling them. The only thing Dad hates more than eye rolling is back talk. "Abigail, Kane, Mark. Some other people." I lead with Abigail, because before now, I've never hung out with guys I wasn't dating. Except... now I *am* dating Kane. I bite my lower lip to hide my smile.

"Kane," Dad says thoughtfully. "Is that the one you were at the beach with not long ago?"

"Yes, Dad. He's my partner in foods class."

A small smile forms on Dad's lips, and I'm afraid of what he'll say next. I hate talking about boys with my dad, it's so awkward. "Well," he says. "I'm glad you had fun."

I wait a beat, anticipating the next line of questioning. Dad returns to his newspaper, and I realize that's it. The interrogation is over. Slowly, I stand and head back toward the stairs. I pause before exiting the room, glancing back at Dad. He's absorbed in his paper. This whole thing was weird, but I'm hoping that smile on his face is a sign that the therapy idea has been scrapped.

Once locked in my room with my makeup removed and my PJ's on, I lay back in bed. I flip my sketchpad open to Kane's portrait and trace the edges of his face with my finger and smile.

What was I afraid of? It's been weeks and, aside from my normal aches and pains, I've been flare up free. Maybe I can do this. Maybe I won't be a burden on Kane or Abigail.

I have an urge to do something nice for Kane, so I flip to a clean page in my sketch pad. I unlock my phone lock screen and pull up a recent selfie I snapped of Kane and me. He looks adorable, flashing the camera his trademark grin, and I actually look happy. I realize now that I *was* happy then, and I've actually been mostly happy for a while now.

Inhaling deeply, I get to work. My gaze flicks between the phone and the paper, as I sketch the outline of first Kane, then me. After a while I lean back, resting my eyes for a short break.

When I open them again, the sun is filtering through my bedroom window. Blinking, I realize I slept through the entire night. The sketchpad is still open beside me, the pencil dangerously close to my face.

Groaning, I sit up and stretch. My joints are stiff and achy. I place the pencil next to the sketchpad and find my phone half buried under the paper, the notification light blinking at me.

Once I clear the low battery warning, I glance at the clock— 9:43 a.m.—and see an unread text from Kane. Before I can open it, the battery reaches critical, and the phone shuts down. I groan and connect my phone to the charger, then I take a bundle of fresh clothes into the bathroom and step into the shower. The water works wonders on my joints.

I towel off and dress, then apply a fresh bandage over my tattoo. It could be just from the warmth of the shower, but it looks more red and puffy this morning.

Brush in hand, I return to my room and see that my phone has enough juice to read the text. *You + Me = Picnic?*

I smile, setting down the hairbrush, and send back a quick reply. *Yes. When?*

His reply is almost instantaneous. *11?*

Sitting on the front steps, skin coated in a fresh layer of extra strong sunscreen, I wave goodbye as Mom pulls out of the driveway. She's taking Mandy to piano lessons, and Dad is at the office prepping for court on Monday. This leaves me alone to wait for Kane. Thank god. I'm still not ready for my parents to meet him.

He rolls up on his bike, and I meet him at the end of the driveway. He's wearing khaki shorts and carrying a black backpack on his shoulders. I smile at his t-shirt. It says, "Exercise? I Thought You Said Extra Fries!"

"Your chariot awaits," he says, gesturing grandly to his bicycle's handlebars. "And for the record, I have a 99 percent passenger satisfaction rating."

"Only 99 percent?" I raise my eyebrows and climb on, then swivel my head to face him.

He shrugs. "I gave Mark a ride on the handlebars once when we were ten. We hit a pothole, he fell off. He's refused to ever ride with me again."

I laugh, and the grin on his face only fuels my mirth. When my laughter settles down, I face forward, bracing myself for the ride. After a few seconds, when we still haven't moved, I turn to face him. "What are we waiting for?"

"I don't work for free." His face is dead serious.

My jaw drops, and a sharp laugh escapes me. "Excuse me?"

"You heard me." The grin creeps back onto his face, and he points at his left cheek. Rolling my eyes, I close the space between us and plant a quick kiss on his skin.

"Can we go now?"

"As you wish." His take off is a bit wobbly, but soon it's smooth riding until we reach the beach boardwalk. He chains up his bike, and we walk hand in hand toward our rocky cliff. He helps me up the slope, and down the other side to the secret beach. I'm happy to see it's as deserted now as it was the first time he brought me here.

I stand for a moment in the middle of the beach, taking in our surroundings with a smile on my face. In my peripheral, I see Kane dump the backpack onto the sand and pull out a huge beach towel. He tries to lay it out, but the breeze coming off the ocean refuses to comply.

"Need a hand?" I grab the opposite end of the towel, and we manage to spread it flat.

"Thanks," Kane says. He gestures to the towel. "Ladies first."

Grinning, I sit cross legged and Kane follows suit. He pulls the backpack closer and pulls out assorted plastic containers.

"Uh..." He stares into the bag, then looks up at me with wide eyes.

"What?" I ask, my voice cautious.

He blushes, and it makes him look young. "You're not opposed to eating potato salad with your hands, are you?"

"What?" I say again, this time in surprise.

He flashes me a sheepish smile.

I close my eyes, shaking my head and laughing. "Hands it is."

23

KANE

A breath of relief escapes me. With some other girl, forgetting the utensils for this picnic could have been a complete disaster. It would be just my luck to get dumped for something so dumb less than 24 hours after becoming official. But Summer laughed it off. I knew it the instant she first spared me a second glance, but every moment I spend with this amazing girl just reminds me that I'm the luckiest guy in the world.

I pop the lid of the grapes open, reach in, and pop a couple in my mouth. Summer, sitting only two feet away, reaches into her cactus purse and pulls out a travel bottle of hand sanitizer.

"Smart idea," I say, offering her my palms. She squirts some onto my skin and I rub my hands together. I reach for the food.

"Wait!" she cries.

I cock my head to the side in question, my hand paused above the grapes.

"Let it dry, you dork." She rolls her eyes. "Hand sanitizer tastes nasty."

"Smart and beautiful."

She tips her face down, hiding behind her shield of hair. I take advantage of the moment and scoot across the towel, so my knees are touching hers. I place my hand under her chin and tip her face up, forcing her eyes to meet mine.

"Smart and beautiful," I repeat. Her already pink cheeks brighten, but she holds my gaze. I smile at her, then press my lips gently to hers for just a moment. "You'd better get used to the compliments."

"Compliments, accidents, and forgetfulness." She narrows her eyes. "That's what I signed up for?"

"And bad jokes." I glance at the food behind me. "Are my hands ready?"

She nods once. Grabbing the container of grapes, I pull one off the stem and turn to her. "Open up." She obeys, and I place it in her mouth.

"Thanks," she says, smiling. Her gaze flicks to the assorted containers spread out. "Hand me the potato salad?"

"As you wish," I say, using the infamous line from *The Princess Bride,* which I remember was in her top five. Then I reach out and grab the container. I hand it to her, and she removes the lid, setting it carefully aside.

"Open up," she echoes my earlier words.

I do as she commands and watch her dip two fingers into the potato salad. I wait for her to bring the food to my waiting mouth.

She pauses six inches from my face, and her lower lip finds its way between her teeth.

I open my mouth and say, "Ahhh," as though I'm a baby, waiting for the choo-choo train spoon to enter the tunnel.

She smiles, rolls her eyes, and slips her fingers into my mouth. My teeth close against her fingers in a gentle bite, and she jerks back, smearing potato salad all over my chin. We both burst into laughter.

"Jerk!" But I know she doesn't mean it. She's smiling too much.

The rest of our picnic is lighthearted and fun, with only a few more minor food accidents. When we're done, we kick off our shoes, and walk down to the water's edge to rinse our hands and faces.

"Hey, Kane," Summer says, leaning over and rubbing her hands together in the water.

I look at her. "Yeah?"

"Think fast!" She whips her hands out of the water, sending a spray of salt water at me.

Laughing, I immediately crouch close to the water and retaliate, sending my own shower of water.

She splashes back, and for a minute we have a small water fight.

Standing, she shields her face and laughs, as I send a big splash at her. "No more!" she cries.

"You started it." I shrug, the grin on my face so huge it almost hurts. I reach out for her hand. "Truce?"

She accepts my peace offering, and together we return to our belongings.

"A picnic was a good idea," she says, drying herself on the big towel.

"I'm full of ideas," I reply. "A few of them are bound to be good."

She laughs, and it's music to my ears.

I lean over and place a kiss to her lips. Ideas for our next date are already spinning in my mind.

Two weeks have passed since Summer and I became official. Two full weeks of getting to see her and kiss her every day, even weekends. In other words, these have been the best two weeks of my life. The only thing that would make it better is if she'd show me her tattoo.

The line for dance tickets winds down the hall and around the corner from the cafeteria. I wait with Mark, impatiently shifting my weight from one foot to the other. How long does it take to buy a ticket...and why isn't the line moving?

"Dude, chill," Mark says, when he's finally had enough of my fidgeting.

"Sorry," I mutter, forcing my body to still. I busy myself with people watching. My gaze skims over the familiar faces. These are the people I've seen every day for the last two years, some longer. I know most by face, if not name, but I wouldn't say any are really my friends. Mark and Abigail are the only people I hang out with. They get me.

"Where's Abz?" I ask.

"Eating lunch."

"Why isn't she here buying her ticket?"

"She threw scissors to my paper. I have to buy her ticket." He shakes his head, but he's smiling. I laugh.

Mark's attention drifts behind me, and I follow his gaze and frown. Summer exits a room and hastily slinks down the hall away from us. She's out of sight before the door can fully close behind her.

"I wonder why Summer was in the nurse's office," I muse. She's moved out of my line of sight, so I turn back to Mark.

"Probably a headache or something."

"Right," I agree, but even as I say it, I don't believe it. Most kids at school smuggle their own over-the-counter headache contraband in their bags.

We make it to the front of the line and purchase two tickets each. After a quick stop in the cafeteria for food, we finally arrive at our usual lunch table. Abigail and Summer are already seated, deep in conversation.

"What's new?" I ask, as I sling my arm around Summer's shoulders.

She smiles at me. "Nothing since yesterday."

I scrutinize her for any sign of illness, but she's as perfect as ever. Narrowing her eyes, she swipes her hand across her mouth.

"Do I have food on my face?"

"Huh? No."

"Then why are you staring at me like that?"

"I just like to look at you."

She blushes, and as always, hides behind her hair. "How much do I owe you for the ticket?"

"Nothing. I asked you, I'm paying."

"One of these days you have to let me pay for something."

I grin, but keep my mouth shut. I want to give her the world, but my savings are starting to dwindle. I might have to take her up on her offer to pay. Or get a job.

Across the table, Mark turns to Abigail. "Twenty bucks."

"Pardon?" Abigail cocks an eyebrow at him.

"I'm not your boyfriend. I stood in line, but you still need to pay up. Our deal was that I would *get* your ticket, not pay for it."

She rolls her eyes. "Semantics. Fine. I'll pay you back this weekend. Though, maybe Kane should be paying for us, since *he's* the reason we're even going."

I hold my hands up defensively. "Nope. That was not a condition when you agreed."

In foods class, I study Summer's profile as Ms. Knope explains some assignment we're supposed to work on. Something about nutrients, I think. I'm too distracted to give class even half my attention. There's still no sign that anything is the matter with Summer, besides her usual sleepiness. I suppose she does look a little paler than normal. Maybe she's anemic? I think anemia causes exhaustion. And paleness?

"You're staring again," Summer whispers out of the corner of her mouth.

I reach over and give her arm a gentle squeeze. "Wanna hang out after school?" I ask, keeping my voice pitched low.

Her eyes stay focused on the front of the room as she whispers, "As much as I'd love to, I really need to catch up on homework."

"We can study," I insist.

She tilts her face toward mine and smiles. "Next time."

I nod, disappointed. I know I've been monopolizing her lately, and my own homework has been suffering. Maybe she has a point. Besides, if we studied together, I'd probably end up studying *her* and not my textbooks.

The memory of seeing her leaving the nurse's office is still nagging at me. I want to ask, but I know her well enough now to know she'll be evasive.

24

SUMMER

My head is pounding. My joints are aching. My cheeks hurt from the fake smile I've been wearing all day. As much as I'd love to spend another afternoon with Kane, my body is screaming for my bed. I'm simply out of spoons.

It feels like another flare up is on the way. I've been running myself ragged between Kane and school. I thought I was doing better, but it's all catching up to me.

As soon as I arrive home from school, I kick off my shoes, not bothering to put them on the shoe rack.

On my way to my room for a nap, my phone buzzes in the back pocket of my jeans. I pull it out and smile at the screen. Kane has sent me a meme of a cheese grater with a block of cheese. It reads, "This might sound cheesy...but I think you're really grate."

I send back a heart emoji, then turn my screen off and lay down on my bed.

When my eyes open again, my bedroom is dark. I can vaguely recall my sister trying to wake me for dinner. Unless that was a dream, I remember rolling over, hiding my face beneath my pillow, and mumbling for her to go away.

Feeling disoriented, I feel around for my phone. I tap a button, bringing the screen to life, and cringe away from the brightness. I squint at the screen, tapping until I've brought the brightness level all the way down. Then I look at the clock. 3 am. Wonderful. And I missed my evening meds.

Clicking the screen off, I roll onto my back and squeeze my eyes shut. No matter how hard I try, though, I can't fall back to sleep. So I lay there in the dark, staring at my ceiling, thinking about how awful and exhausting today will be. Sure I got almost twelve hours of sleep, they just weren't during the hours I needed them most.

The seconds tick by.

Minutes.

Hours.

Sleep remains elusive.

I'm yawning when my alarm goes off, and any chance of sleeping is long gone. I'm not missing school over this. I refuse to let my disease win. Besides, it's Thursday. I can make it through two more days of school.

My body is sore and aching when I force myself out of bed and through my morning routine. A hot shower helps loosen my joints. The skin around my tattoo seems redder now than it was yesterday, and I hope I'm imagining it in my sleep deprived state. Despite a heavy hand with my concealer, the dark shadows under my eyes remain. I look less like a zombie, but anyone looking close enough will be able to see something isn't right. And I know Kane will be looking closely, he always is.

School is as painful as I imagined it would be. It's a struggle to keep my eyes open, and I actually nod off while sitting upright in chemistry. I startle myself fully awake when I nearly tumble off my lab stool.

I must look really awful, because Mark shadows me in the hall from chemistry to my English class. He stays far enough back so it's not obvious he's following me, but I've never seen him take this path between classes before.

I try to pay attention to my friends at lunch, but I'm still out of it. I force myself to smile, and I nod when appropriate, but mostly I stay quiet.

"You okay?" Kane wraps his arm around my shoulders and whispers in my ear, while Abigail and Mark bicker about something across the table from us.

I nod, pushing my broccoli around on my lunch tray. I'm too tired to even eat.

Kane gives my arm a squeeze. Though I'm sure it's obvious I'm lying, he doesn't press. "Can you hang out after school, or do you have more homework?"

I shake my head. "Sorry, I really can't today."

And I mean that. As much as I do love spending time with him, I physically can't keep up my act for longer than the school day. Hell, I don't know if I'll even last until the final bell rings. I'm already struggling to stay awake.

We finish lunch and Kane grabs my bag and empty lunch tray without asking, then takes my hand and helps me to stand. He wraps his arm around my shoulders, and I lean on him as we ditch the tray and walk to foods class. I hope we don't get called out by any of the teachers for PDA, because remaining upright is much easier with his assistance.

All through foods, I can feel Kane's eyes on me. I struggle to keep my own eyes open, but knowing he's watching me is a good motivator. I stare at Ms. Knope, though most of what she says is lost to me. I hope Kane is paying attention and taking mental notes, but I have a feeling he's only paying attention to me.

When class ends, he walks me to my final class.

"You're sure you're okay?" he asks, pitching his voice low so that our classmates have less chance of overhearing.

I nod once.

Kane looks like he wants to say something, but he seems to think better of it. He lifts my hand and places a kiss on my knuckles. "I'll text you later."

I nod again, watching him retreat down the hall. He looks back once, and I give him a weak wave. One more class, that's all I need to endure, and then I can go home and sleep.

I zone out during my final class, watching the clock more than my teacher. The final bell rings, and I exhale a relieved breath. I made it. I don't even bother stopping by my locker. I move as quickly as my leaden legs will allow and board the school bus.

When I arrive home, it's a repeat of yesterday. I immediately climb in bed, but this time I manage to rouse myself for dinner when Mandy comes charging into my room. I push my food around my plate, trying to eat, but it's too much work to lift the fork to my mouth and chew. Eventually, I give up and stare at my spaghetti.

"Summer, honey, are you feeling okay?"

Mom's voice pulls my attention from my plate, and I meet her worried gaze. I nod silently. "Just tired."

She hesitates for a moment. "Well, if you're not going to eat, why don't you head to bed. I'll take care of your plate."

"Thanks, Mom."

I must look awful if she's going to clear my plate for me. When I reach my room, I crash for the night.

When I wake, I feel better rested than yesterday, but I'm still nowhere near 100 percent. Even after my shower, I feel feverish, so I sneak to the medicine cabinet and steal the thermometer. Sitting cross legged on my bed, I slip it under my tongue and wait. When I remove it, I stare at the thermometer and silently curse the reading.

I always run a low-grade fever, but this is higher than normal. I don't think I'm in dangerous territory though. Not yet anyway.

I hear movement outside my bedroom door, followed by three taps. I quickly shove the thermometer under my pillow, and call, "Come in." This is probably nothing. I'm going to school and I'll be fine.

"How are you feeling this morning?" Mom asks, poking her head in my room.

I shrug. "Better than yesterday." Not a total lie.

"Do you need to stay home? I can call school, and you can rest today."

"No, I'm fine, Mom. I'll go to the nurse if I need to."

Mom studies me for a moment, then decides to believe me. "Okay, honey. Have a good day."

"You too, Mom."

I quickly run my brush through my hair and apply my lip gloss. The urge to peel back the fresh gauze over my tattoo is strong, but I'm sure nothing has changed since I last checked. I wonder if Abigail's tattoo is the same. I shake my head and adjust my clothes. Grabbing my backpack, I exit my room, slamming the door shut behind me.

I feel no worse when I get to school, so I count that as a win. Homeroom is a snooze, and I'm eager to get through the first half of the day and to lunch. I've never told him, but I'll always be grateful to Kane for talking to me at lunch that first day of school. I was resigned to finishing high school with no friends, and despite my reluctance to open up to him, Kane refused to let that happen. The last time I was as happy as I've been these last few weeks was before I got sick and received my diagnosis.

Deep down though, I know this will blow up in my face. Kane is amazing. He's funny and sweet and kind. He's always opening doors for me and carrying my backpack. He deserves better than what I can give him. I should've stopped this before it even started. But I'm too selfish for that. I like being with him. And I know that he's going to get hurt in the end. And it'll be my fault.

When I stop at my locker between first and second period, I'm hit with a wave of dizziness. Head resting against the cool locker, I take a few deep breaths, while I try to pull myself together. I'm fine. I have to be fine. Exhaling slowly, I open my locker and exchange my books, then set off for chemistry. I'm still a little dizzy, but I refuse to let it stop me. I will not let my disease win.

I stumble onto my lab stool, the metal scraping loudly across the linoleum floor. Ducking my head, I hide behind my hair. The last thing I want to do is draw attention to myself, and what do I do? I go and trip over my own stool.

Smooth Summer, real smooth.

I cross my arms over the surface of the lab table and rest my head. I've broken out into a cool sweat, and I can feel a rush of chills coming on. My body alternates between waves of heat and shivers.

This can't be happening. Not here. Not now. I try to breathe deep and slow. *Mind over matter. I will be okay. I will be fine.*

But I'm not fine.

When Mr. Garrison begins taking attendance, I raise my head and another wave of dizziness washes over me. I squeeze my eyes closed and grip the edge of my table. My lab partner, Miguel, probably thinks I'm insane.

I listen to the names of my classmates being called out and wait for my own name.

"Marisa Roberts," Mr. Garrison's voice floats across the room. I hear Marisa call out "Here" and then my name is called.

"Here," I say in a shaky voice.

Instead of moving on, Mr. Garrison pauses, his eyes fixed on me, a frown on his face.

"Are you feeling all right, Summer?" he asks.

I nod my head weakly. I just need to make it through this class. Then I can go visit Nurse Hill and lay down in her office until I feel better.

Mr. Garrison looks skeptical, but he moves on to the next name on the list, and I let out a relieved breath. I can already feel too many eyes on me. When I glance around the room, the owners of those eyes all turn away, except for Mark. He's watching me from the table across the aisle, his brow creased. I give him a forced smile then train my eyes on the front of the room.

I have a difficult time concentrating. My classmates stand, and I figure out a beat too late what's going on. They're heading toward the cabinets in the back of the room to gather equipment for today's lab.

Hands braced on the counter, I stand and take a step toward the back of the room. And then it hits me. The world is spinning, it's like being stuck in an undertow, unable to gather my bearings and distinguish up from down. My vision goes black. Before I know what's happening, the ground is rising up to meet me.

My brain is so foggy, I don't even feel the impact when I hit the floor. I hear scattered gasps and cries, but everything sounds muffled and far away.

When I open my eyes, my cheek is against the gratefully cool floor, and Mark's face comes into view. His eyes are wide, his forehead creased with...is that worry? He's frowning.

He says something, but I can't focus. I blink, trying to stop the room from spinning. Mark repeats himself, and this time I understand.

"Summer, did you hit your head?"

I shake my head. "I'm okay."

There's a hint of a smile on Mark's lips. "You are far from okay, Summer." Then his hands are under me, and he's scooping me into his arms.

Mr. Garrison appears before me.

"Get her to the nurse's office," Garrison says. "Grab a pass on your way back."

Mark nods his head once, and then we're moving.

"You're hot, Summer," Mark says softly, once we're alone in the hall.

Wait, is he hitting on me right now? I scrunch my brow at him.

His neck flushes pink, and he says, "I think you have a fever. You're burning up."

"Let me walk." He's still carrying me in his arms as we head toward the office.

"Not a chance. Last time you tried to stand you fainted."

I don't have the energy to argue, so I relax in his arms and silently wait for the short walk to the office to end. I feel ridiculous, like a little kid. But he has a fair point, I'm so weak and dizzy, I'm not sure I'd be able to walk on my own.

We arrive at the office and, because his arms are full, Mark kicks the door to knock.

"Summer!" Nurse Hill exclaims, when she opens the door. Her dark eyes are wide. After a brief moment of shock at seeing me carried to her office, she gestures Mark inside. "Lay her on the cot."

Mark obeys, and I close my eyes and wait in silence while he explains what happened. I hear Nurse Hill rustling around in the cupboards. Her footsteps grow closer, and she tells me to open up. Eyes still closed, I do as she commands and close my lips around the smooth thermometer she's placed under my tongue.

"Oh, sweetie." Nurse Hill's voice is full of concern. She knows about my health issues, if she sounds worried, I know I must be in trouble. "Mr. Traeger, please return to class."

"I need a hall pass."

I honestly don't think Mark gives a shit about having a hall pass. I open my eyes, and I can see the worry on his face. A sudden panic overcomes me. He's going to tell Kane. And Abigail. And then all my new friends will know just how broken I am. I never should have agreed to go out with Kane. I should have sent him packing on day one.

Nurse Hill sighs then turns back to me. She removes the thermometer from my mouth, and I close my eyes again, bracing myself for the bad news. "Summer, your fever is 103.6. We need to bring this down. Do you have any other symptoms?"

"I'm really dizzy," I whisper, "and I have chills and hot flashes off and on."

She's busying herself pulling an ice pack from the little freezer under her desk. She wraps it in a towel and places it across my forehead. It's freezing, and my body begins to convulse with shivers, but I know we need to bring the fever down, so I suck it up and keep my complaints to myself.

"Anything else, Summer? Any new rashes or other aches and pains?"

I bite my lip, wondering if I should mention my tattoo. It probably shouldn't be red and swollen anymore. Despite trying to convince myself this is normal, the Internet told me it's probably not.

"Anything at all?"

Painfully aware that Mark is still in the room, I push up the hem of my shirt and fold down the waistband of my shorts. Peeling back the gauze, I reveal the little dragonfly.

Mark sucks in a sharp breath. He's tall enough that he has a clear view, even though he's standing behind Nurse Hill, looking over her shoulder.

"How long ago did you get that?" she asks.

I shrug. "A few weeks."

Nurse Hill reaches out a hand, touches the tattoo, and shakes her head. "It's definitely infected."

I close my eyes, trying to hold in my tears. I know what an

infection means. My body is creating an overabundance of antibodies, attacking not only the infection, but my whole body.

"I'm calling your parents."

I groan. So much for keeping the tattoo a secret. If the infection doesn't kill me, my parents just might.

25

KANE

W hat do you mean Summer is sick?"
   I stare at Mark, dumbfounded, as he tells me what happened in chemistry class. If I wasn't so surprised by his words, I'd be pissed that he didn't track me down and tell me as soon as it happened. Or at least text me.

Mark sighs. "I mean—" He pauses and gives me an impatient look. "— she had a fever above 103 and the nurse called her parents to come pick her up."

As I listen to Mark's words, I stare at my phone in disbelief. Why hasn't Summer called or texted if she's sick? Or maybe she's *too* sick? That would be worse.

"You're 100 percent sure?" Mark isn't a liar, but I have to ask. Sure, Summer seemed really tired yesterday, but I chalked that up to her staying up too late the night before catching up on homework. Then again, I did see her leaving the nurses' office the other day. And she *does* have a habit of keeping secrets from everyone. But, why wouldn't she say something if she wasn't feeling well?

Mark glares. "Why would I lie about this, Kane?"

My shoulders slump in defeat, and I stab at a cold macaroni

noodle in the plastic container in front of me—leftovers from dinner last night.

"Lie about what?" Abigail sets her tray down next to Mark and looks between the two of us.

"Summer's tattoo is infected," Mark explains.

"That sucks," she replies, flipping open the cap on her reusable water bottle and taking a drink.

I glare at her. Summer wouldn't have the tattoo *or* the infection if it wasn't for Abigail.

"It's not *just* an infection," I spit at her. "She fainted in class. She has a fever and who knows what else."

"Damn." Abigail draws the word out, sounding more compassionate than she had a moment before.

"You just had to get her involved in that stupid tattoo plan of yours, didn't you?"

"Chill out, Kane," Mark interjects. He's always the voice of reason, and right now I hate that. "This is *not* Abigail's fault."

I bite my tongue and scowl at my so-called friends. I know if I keep talking, I'm going to regret what comes out of my mouth. Mark holds my gaze, and finally I avert my stare to my cold macaroni. I snap the lid on the container and toss it into the brown paper bag. Standing, I throw one last glare at my friends before storming back into the school.

I don't know where I'm going, I just know that I'm worried about Summer and I have to be moving. I wish I had my skateboard, but I do the next best thing; I wander the halls hoping to blow off some steam. Somehow, I manage to avoid any of the school staff, so I don't get in trouble for wandering the halls without a pass.

Before long, I find myself outside the nurse's office. Without knocking, I pull open the door and poke my head in. Nurse Hill looks up from her desk.

"Mr. Dwyer, what can I do for you?"

I open my mouth to speak then hesitate. Finally, I close the door behind me. "What's wrong with Summer?"

She gives me a small smile. "I can't give out information about other students."

"She's not just some other student," I insist. "She's my *girlfriend*."

"I'm sorry, Kane, but that doesn't change the fact that I can't tell you anything. Give her a call tomorrow, okay?"

Shoulders slumped in defeat, I turn back to the door and grasp the handle. I slowly push the door open, and she begins to speak again. I freeze.

"I wouldn't worry too much," she offers. "She's in good hands."

I exit the office and stand in the empty hall a moment before continuing my wandering.

When the bell rings, my feet carry me to the foods classroom. I sink into my seat and stare at my hands which are fisted on the table.

"Hey."

I look up, hoping the feminine voice speaking is Summer, but I know it's not even before I look up into Rachel's face.

"Hey." I return to staring at my hands. I'm not in the mood for small talk.

"Um," Rachel continues, not taking the hint. Or maybe just not caring. Out of the corner of my eye I see her weight shifting from foot to foot. She tucks a strand of black hair behind her ear. She's clearly uncomfortable about this confrontation. "I heard something happened to Summer in class earlier. You're with her now, right? Is she okay?"

I glance at her again and shrug.

"Right, look, I don't know what she's said about me, but she was my best friend for a long time. I still care about her, even if she never wants to see me again. Will you just tell me if she's seriously hurt or sick?"

"Your guess is as good as mine." The words come out more vicious than I intend. I take a deep breath and let it out, trying to calm myself before I piss her off. "Sorry. I just don't know any more than you do. I haven't talked to her since yesterday, and she was fine then. Tired, but fine."

She bites her lip again, and I avert my eyes. Summer always bites her lip when she's nervous.

"You seem like a nice guy, Kane, so I feel like I should warn you about her."

"What?" I demand, again more harshly than she probably deserves.

She flinches but continues. "After she got mono last spring, she completely ghosted me. *And* the guy she was dating. Like, not returning texts or phone calls, not letting anyone visit her. Completely off the radar. When she came back to school, she quit the volleyball team and the debate club. She quit talking to *everyone*."

"Why are you telling me this?"

"Like I said, you seem like a nice guy. And..." she hesitates, the lip finding its way between her teeth again. "I think you're good for her. Just don't be surprised if she disappears on you too."

I stare blankly at her. I can't even fathom Summer ghosting me like she did to Rachel. After a moment of silence, Rachel gets the hint that I'm not in a talking mood and returns to her own table.

Ms. Knope begins class, but my focus is gone. All I can do is worry about Summer.

While my wrist was in the cast, I imagined spending all my free time on my board. I wasn't going to squander a single moment that could be spent skating. Funny how quickly things change.

It's another California perfect Sunday afternoon, and I'm

spending it warming the bench, while Mark and Abigail skate around me. It's like I've gone back in time to a few weeks ago, except now I'm sitting here by choice. Well, sort of.

I just want to go home. Stare at my screen. And use my Jedi mind powers to make Summer reply to any of the unanswered texts I've sent since lunch on Friday. But Mark and Abigail wouldn't take no for an answer.

"She'll call you when she's feeling better," Mark says, skating to a stop in front of me. I realize I've been staring at my blank screen again.

"When I'm sick, I don't want to do anything or talk to anyone," Abigail adds, pulling up to a stop beside Mark. I know she thinks she's being helpful, but I was hoping I wasn't just *anyone* to Summer. I was hoping I was important enough to call even when she was sick.

I force a smile, and my friends skate off. I do a quick Internet search for another meme to cheer Summer up. I find one of a stick of butter with a sad face that says, "Get Butter Soon." I type, *I hope you're feeling better*, and hit send.

I stare at the screen, willing a reply to come through. I'm ready to quit holding my breath when the tell-tale bubbles appear. Summer is typing something. But then the bubbles disappear, and no message comes through.

Defeated, I shove my phone in my pocket and grab my board. I leave without saying goodbye.

26

SUMMER

I'm grounded.

My parents didn't take away my phone. I thought for sure that would be the first phase of my punishment when we got home from the hospital, but it wasn't. I kind of wish they had though, at least then I wouldn't have to see all the sweet and funny texts Kane is sending.

Sitting cross legged on my bed I stare at his latest text. The butter meme stares back at me, with Kane's concerned message.

I hate that my initial resolve of solitude crumbled so quickly under his persistence. I never should have agreed to go out with him. I never should have said yes to going to Homecoming, and especially not when he asked me to be his girlfriend. Without me in his life, he'd happily be riding around on his skateboard. Probably breaking more bones but doing it with a smile on his face.

Biting my lower lip, I try to decide whether or not to reply. I haven't replied to any of his texts or voicemails yet, and the guilt is eating at me. I'm the worst girlfriend ever.

A little better. Still not 100%, I tap the message on the screen.

Before I can hit send, my bedroom door cracks open and Mandy pokes her little blonde head in. "Wanna play Minecraft with me?" She keeps her voice soft, as though speaking at a normal volume may shatter me. *Too late little sis, I'm already broken.*

I give her a small smile. "Not right now, Mandy. Sorry."

"Oh...okay." I hear the disappointment in her voice, but I don't stop her when she quietly closes the door and leaves.

I stare at the screen again and re-read my message. Shaking my head, I delete the unsent text and swipe back to the home screen. My background image, a photo I snapped of Kane and me at the beach the night he asked me to be his girlfriend, mocks me. I throw my phone on the bed, screen down. Pulling out my sketch pad, I flip to a blank page and begin something new.

I get lost in my sketch and lose track of time. I'm startled by a knock on my bedroom door. A quick glance at the clock on my phone tells me it's been well over an hour since Mandy's last appearance. Tossing the phone back on the bed, I ignore the knock and pick up my pencil once more. I glance up when my parents enter, then return my attention to my artwork.

"Summer," Dad says, his deep, lawyer voice demands my attention.

Reluctantly, I set aside my sketchpad and look at him. His face is neutral, the same face I imagine he uses during cross examinations in the courtroom.

I knew it was only a matter of time before they had this chat with me. My tattoo—and subsequent infection—has been the elephant in the room since Nurse Hill called my mom. Dad had been in court and met us at the hospital as soon as he'd heard. From my hospital bed I'd heard them arguing in the hall. Dad wanted to read me the riot act right then and there. Mom made him promise to wait until I was feeling better and they'd had time to cool down and talk things out together. Apparently, that moment had come.

"Was it worth it?" Mom asks, perching on the edge of my bed. I shift my gaze from Dad to her. She looks sad.

I shrug.

"That's not an answer, Summer," Dad says sternly.

I fight back the tears welling up in my eyes and finally manage to speak. "I just wanted to do something normal."

"Getting a tattoo in some guy's basement when you are still a minor is not *normal*!" I flinch at Dad's outburst.

"It wasn't a basement..." I mutter and instantly regret it.

"I don't care if it was a legitimate tattoo shop," Dad exclaims. "The fact of the matter is, you made a huge mistake. Immune disease or not, you should never have done it. I thought you were smarter than this."

I stare at my lap, unable to meet his disappointed gaze. From the corner of my eye, I see Mom place a gentle hand on his arm.

"Summer, we know you want to just fit in," she said. "But we need you to think about your health first. It's one thing to spend a day at the beach, if you're smart and use sunscreen and seek shade. It's another to do something like *this*, something with such a high risk of infection."

"I did my research, you know," I say loudly, looking back and forth between my parents. "Plenty of people with lupus get tattoos."

Dad's eyes are blazing, and I look away again.

"But sweetie," Mom says. "They get tattoos in legitimate tattoo shops that have health inspectors, not random guys apartments. Did he even use sterile needles?"

I can't answer that, because I don't know. I wasn't paying that close of attention.

"You don't have to worry," I tell them. "I'm not going to be hanging out with those friends anymore anyway."

"We don't want you to give up your friends," Mom says. Her voice is full of pain. "We just want you to make smarter decisions."

I don't say anything. They soon get the hint that I'm not going to add anything more to this conversation and leave me alone.

I stay locked up in my room all evening. When Mandy comes

to get me for dinner, I tell her I'm not hungry and she goes away. By the time the house is silent, and everyone has gone to bed, I'm starving. I sneak to the kitchen and make myself a snack. Grabbing the pills I didn't take with dinner, I return to my room before anyone can catch me.

Gently closing my bedroom door, I lean against it and close my eyes. When I open them, my gaze lands on the blue dress hanging on my closet door. Homecoming is in less than a week. I'm not going, and I have yet to break the news to Kane. I'm the worst girlfriend ever. And soon to be no girlfriend at all.

27

KANE

I've just sent Summer an incredibly cheesy meme of two chocolate bunnies, each with a bite taken out of them, when Mom claims my attention.

"Kane!"

I look up, and I feel a little guilty. She's wearing that exasperated look again. She must've been trying to get my attention for a while.

"Put the phone away at the dinner table."

I check my screen once more and see that Summer has seen my message. I hold my breath and wait for her reply, even though she hasn't replied to a single text, voicemail, GIF, or emoji I've sent since the day she left school sick. I glance once more at Mom, still giving me *The Look*, and I set the phone down on the table beside my plate. "Sorry."

She gives me a sad, knowing smile. "Summer?"

I nod.

She frowns. "I'm sorry, honey."

I cut a large piece off the chicken breast on my plate and shove it in my mouth. Mom and I have already talked about my lack of contact with my girlfriend. This is my way of saying I'm done with the topic. Summer has missed school all week, and her parents won't let her have any visitors. Worst of all, the Homecoming dance is tomorrow.

"Anyway," Mom says, her voice brightening. "Are you excited to see your dad next weekend?"

Sill chewing the chicken, I nod, thankful for the change in subject.

"Do you two have any big plans?"

I swallow and say, "Bungee jumping."

Mom gives me a wary look and I grin.

"Kidding, Mom." I pause. "We're saving that for my eighteenth birthday."

She rolls her eyes. "You two will be the death of me."

"He's taking me camping," I tell her, trying to ease her worry.

"That should be fun. But please use the marked trails, don't go running off making your own."

I shrug. "Sure."

I know she doesn't believe me, but camping is a lot safer than bungee jumping, so she lets it go.

We finish our meal, making small talk, then I retreat to my bedroom. I stare at my phone again, willing a reply to appear with just the power of my mind. Clearly The Force is not with me, as the screen remains blank.

I'm sick of waiting around. I need to see her.

I run back to the kitchen where Mom has just finished cleaning up dinner. "I'm running out for a bit. I'll be back soon."

Mom dismisses me with a wave of her hand, and I'm out the front door and on my bike before she can think twice.

I pedal fast and hard, eager to make good time to Summer's house. I arrive, pulling to a stop at the end of her driveway. Pausing to catch my breath, I stare up at the house.

I let the bike fall in the grass near the top of the driveway, then walk up the front steps and knock.

Summer's sister, Mandy, opens the door. Well, I assume it's her sister, I've never actually met any member of Summer's family. I peer over her shoulder; I've also never seen the inside of Summer's house. It's a lot fancier than my house, which contains an assortment of items Mom has collected over the years. Summer's house looks like something out of one of the magazines you find in the waiting room at the doctor or dentist. The furniture matches and doesn't look thirty years old. There are no knick knacks sitting around either. I didn't think real people even had houses like this.

"May I help you?" Mandy asks politely.

"Yeah, I'm here to see Summer."

Mandy's eyes light up, and a sly smile crosses her lips. "Are you her *boyfriend?*"

"Yep, I'm Kane." I grin. "You must be Mandy."

"Mmmhmm." Mandy studies me, a thoughtful expression on her face. "You're shorter than her last boyfriend."

This doesn't faze me. At 5'8″ I'm used to guys being taller than me. "I bet I'm funnier though."

"Probably. Bradley was boring. He would never talk to me like this either. I already like you more."

My grin broadens, but before I can say anything, a voice interrupts us. "Kane? What are you doing here?"

I look past Mandy again and finally see Summer. She's adorable in pink cotton PJs, her blonde hair falling loose around her shoulders. For the first time since I've met her, she's not wearing makeup, and she's wearing glasses. She looks younger now, and her cheeks are flushed, but she still looks beautiful.

Summer's eyes meet mine, her mouth falls open, and she quickly jerks the glasses from her face. It's a shame, she looks really cute in them.

"She's still grounded," Mandy informs me. "But Mom and Dad are gone. I won't tell on you." She winks and walks past Summer into another room.

I'm left standing in the doorway with Summer in front of me.

"You can't be here," she says.

I close the door behind me and take one step inside. "I won't stay long. I just wanted to see you in person to make sure you're really okay."

"Well, you've seen me. I'm fine."

I study her closer, there are purple half moons under her eyes. She looks exhausted. Beautiful, but exhausted. I know better than to say anything about this though.

"Are you sure? Is there anything I can do to help?"

She bites her lip, lost in thought for a moment, then says, "Let's sit outside."

She nods toward the door I've just closed, and I open it. "Ladies first." I gesture for her to lead and I follow, closing the door behind us.

Summer takes a seat on the top step of the stoop, and I sit beside her. I glance around, taking in the view of the other houses nearby. A silver Lexus drives past, and I give Summer my full attention. She bites her lip again, her brow furrowed. One of her hands grips the other tightly in her lap.

"Are you really okay?" I ask.

Reaching out, I gently pry her hands apart and squeeze one with mine. I draw circles on the back of her hand with my thumb and wait for her to say anything.

The silence goes on, and finally I say, "Don't feel bad about missing Homecoming. I just want you to get better."

She stares at our hands a moment before pulling hers away.

She still hasn't said anything, and I'm starting to get anxious. "Summer?"

"I can't do this, Kane," she says softly.

I blink at her in confusion, trying to figure out what she's talking about. I open my mouth to say something, but as is common around Summer, I'm at a loss.

Finally, after countless painful seconds go by, I say, "I've already yelled at Abigail. I told her she shouldn't have involved you in the whole tattoo thing."

Summer finally meets my eyes. "It's not her fault. It's mine. I was stupid. I knew better and I just..." Her eyes hold mine, as I wait for her to finish her sentence. "You're a great guy, Kane. Any girl would be lucky to have you. But I just can't be that girl."

She stands abruptly, and before I can even comprehend what she's just said, she's gone. The front door opening and closing behind her before I can stop her. I stare at the door, those few solid inches separating us feel like miles. I'm still trying to make sense of everything she just said, but I think Summer just dumped me.

Finally, I pull myself to my feet and slowly trudge down her front steps. I retrieve my bike from the ground and begin the walk home. I'm too stunned to ride. I don't get far when I change direction, hanging a left toward the beach instead of a right toward home.

When I arrive at my destination, I don't even bother chaining my bike to a rack, instead, I haul it through the sand, find a solitary spot and sit. The gentle ocean waves do nothing to soothe my hurt and confusion.

My mind spins with thoughts of Summer. What could have happened? What did I do to lose the girl of my dreams?

Eventually, the sky becomes so dark I can no longer distinguish between sky and sea, but I know one thing for certain.

I need to come up with a plan to get Summer back.

28

SUMMER

It feels like a piece of me dies when I tell Kane I'm not the girl for him. Knowing that my words are truth isn't enough to stop my heart from shattering into a thousand tiny pieces.

I lean against the door, only a few solid inches separating me from the guy I've somehow fallen head over heels for. The guy whose heart I know I've broken. The guy who is better off without me. I know he'll get over me, find someone new, but I'll always be broken. There's no cure for my disease, and I won't drag him down with me.

The sound of a chair scraping across wood pulls my attention. Mandy must be in the kitchen fixing herself a snack.

Sniffling, I wipe tears from my cheeks with the back of my hand. I hadn't even realized I was crying. I don't want Mandy to see me like this, so I bolt up the stairs to my room, closing the door behind me.

Monday, I have to go back to school and face everyone. I don't know how I'm going to survive. I never should have let anyone get close to me.

Oh, god, I'll have to sit right next to Kane in foods class. Maybe

I'll pretend I'm not feeling well and spend the period with Nurse Hill. Every day. For the rest of the term.

Groaning, I throw myself face first on my bed and scream into my pillow.

Everyone is staring at me. I keep my gaze fixed to the ground in front of me, but I can feel the curious looks burning holes in the back of my head. I'm sure word got around school that I passed out in class. Disappearing for a week afterward only added fuel to the gossip fire, I'm sure.

Spinning the combination on my locker, I try to ignore everyone else. To not let their curiosity bother me. I tune them out and pretend I'm back home, alone, in the sanctity of my bedroom.

"I'm glad you're okay."

I nearly jump out of my skin, spinning around to face the owner of the soft voice behind me. It's Rachel. I inhale a deep breath, bracing myself for another awkward interaction.

"Thanks," I mumble. I turn my back on her again and shove my backpack into the narrow space. I pull out the books I need for my first two classes, catching sight of my reflection in the mirror hanging on the door. My butterfly rash is hidden beneath the makeup I carefully applied this morning, but no amount of makeup can hide the sadness in my eyes.

"You are okay, right?" Rachel hedges.

I turn around again, piercing her with a glare. "I'm fine."

"Okay...well, I'm glad." I expect her to leave, but she continues to stand there, making our interaction even more awkward. "Um, also, I wanted to apologize again for last spring. I never meant to hurt you. It happened so quick, and I know that's no excuse, but I regretted it instantly."

I can't deal with this right now. Or ever. So I turn on my heel and walk toward my first class, which is at the end of the hall. She doesn't follow me, and I'm grateful. If I'm being honest with myself, I don't even care anymore about what happened between her and Bradley. That whole situation is small potatoes compared to everything else that's happened to me since. But the betrayal still hurts, and I don't know if I'm ready to forgive her for it. I don't know if I'll ever be ready for that.

When I reach my classroom door, I risk a glance back. She's still in front of my locker, but she's no longer alone. She's talking to a guy with a stupid haircut I'd recognize anywhere.

My breath catches and my heart plummets when he turns around, his eyes meeting mine.

Kane.

29

KANE

Summer is already standing outside the door to her classroom by the time I reach her locker. I was hoping to talk to her, but instead I'm left standing next to her ex-best friend.

"Is she really okay?" Rachel says, addressing me directly.

I pull my attention from Summer, turning my head and facing the girl beside me. Shrugging, I say, "I don't know."

"How could you not know?" she demands, startling me. This is the first time I've seen her show any emotion besides sadness and defeat.

"She dumped me, okay?" I retort angrily.

Rachel's mouth falls open, the anger draining from her face.

I turn to walk away, but she stops me with two simple words. "I'm sorry."

Without turning to face her again, I storm off down the hall to my own locker and grab my books for class. I need a game plan. I love Summer, and I'm not ready to let her go like this. Not without a real reason for dumping me.

"Still no Summer?" Abigail asks, sliding into her seat at lunch. She turns her head, looking around the courtyard.

"She was in chemistry," Mark offers.

I feel Abigail's eyes on me, but I remain silent, pretending to dig for something in the depths of my bag. I usually tell my friends everything, but I haven't been able to bring myself to tell them about the breakup. The hurt is too fresh. Too deep. So I made excuses to stay home all weekend, avoiding them and the topic of Summer. My and Summer's tickets to homecoming are still sitting on my dresser. I don't think Mark or Abigail went, since Summer and I didn't, but I haven't asked.

"Really, Kane? Nothing to say?" Abigail says.

An irritated sigh, almost a growl, escapes my mouth before I can stop it.

"Whoa..." From the corner of my eye, I see Abigail physically recoil.

"You okay, man?" Mark asks.

I squeeze my eyes shut and take a deep breath. Plastering on a fake grin, I open my eyes and face my friends. "She dumped me, okay?" The words burn like acid on my tongue. "But I'm going to get her back."

Mark and Abigail exchange a doubtful look.

Averting my gaze, I shove my sandwich into my mouth and take a huge bite. I'm not very hungry, but it gives me something to do besides talking to them. I don't think they believe that I'll get Summer back, but they also didn't believe me when I said I'd get her to go out with me in the first place.

I proved them wrong once, I can do it again.

Summer walks into foods class seconds before the bell rings. She hurries to her seat as Ms. Knope closes the door and begins class. I have no doubt Summer planned this so she wouldn't have to talk to me, at least not right away.

I flip open my notebook and angrily rip out a piece of paper. Scrawling on the page, I press my pen so hard the tip nearly rips through the page. Pausing to take a deep breath, I loosen my death grip on the pen.

WHY???

Three little letters are all I write. I slide the paper across the table and stare at her profile, willing her to glance down.

Summer keeps her posture rigid, her attention focused on the front of the room. Her hands are clenched tightly together in her lap under the table, like they were Friday night. I have to restrain myself from reaching out and forcing her grip to relax. I know it won't help anything.

I wait. And wait. But Summer studiously ignores me the entire class period, never so much as glancing at the slip of paper. She lucks out, because there are no partner assignments today, just a lecture. When the bell rings, she's out of her seat and racing for the door before I can even say her name.

I see Rachel watching me, and quickly crumple the sheet of paper into a ball and throw it to the bottom of my backpack. I gather the rest of my things and leave.

The remainder of the week goes by in the same vein as Monday. The tension emanating from Summer in class is almost tangible. I try slipping her a note every day in class, and every day she ignores me.

My already glum mood turns darker with every day that passes. The only bright spot in my future is my upcoming camping trip with Dad. Maybe that'll take my mind off of Summer, and when I get back, I'll have a stroke of genius idea to get her back.

Two honks of a car horn wake me Saturday morning, and I realize I never set my alarm. Rolling out of bed, I find a pair of shorts near my laundry hamper and pull them on in record time.

Not bothering with a shirt or shoes, I race out of my room and through the house. Throwing open the front door, I meet my dad halfway down the driveway. I nearly knock him over when I throw my arms around him, wrapping him in a hug.

I'm probably too old to act like this, but I don't care. Ever since my parents got divorced, this is how I've greeted my dad when he comes to pick me up. I miss seeing him every day, and after this week, I really need him. This camping trip with Dad is the only thing that's kept me going.

"Whoa, Kane!" Dad returns the hug, slapping my back. "Did you just roll out of bed?"

We part and I grin sheepishly. "Maybe..."

Dad laughs and waves a hand in front of his face. "Go brush your teeth kid, your breath stinks. Better grab a shower while you're at it."

When I turn to head back inside, Mom is standing in the front entry. She leans against the door frame, a cup of coffee in each hand.

"Morning, Mom." I give her a peck on the cheek as I stride past her, then hover in the hall for a moment, just out of their sight, eavesdropping.

"Coffee! Thanks, Sarah."

"No problem, Justin. I know you'll need it to keep up with that boy."

Dad laughs, and I smile. I shower quickly and put on clothes that I'm pretty sure are clean, then head back down the hall and enter the kitchen. My parents are still drinking coffee and talking.

Every time I see them together, I wonder why they couldn't work past their differences and stay married. They obviously still care about each other.

"You ready to go, kid," Dad asks, spying me lurking in the doorway.

I shake my head. "No way I'm leaving without food first." I take out the cereal and milk, then add, "And I have to finish packing."

Mom sighs. "Really, Kane? I thought you finished packing yesterday after school."

Just the word *school* makes me think of Summer, and misery replaces the happiness I felt at seeing my dad. I shrug and remain uncharacteristically mute.

Mom and Dad exchange a look, then return to their conversation. I finish pouring my cereal and quickly shovel it into my mouth. When I finish, I leave the dirty dishes in the sink and return to my room to finish packing.

Bag in hand, I grab my phone and charger. I stare at the blank screen for a moment, hoping for a call or text from Summer. After a week of the silent treatment, I know it's not coming.

With a defeated sigh, I shove the phone in my pocket and return to the kitchen.

Dad looks up and beams at me. "Ready to go, kid?"

"Yep, let's hit the road."

I throw my bag on the backseat of the SUV and help Dad attach my bike to the roof rack. I can see the camping gear through the rear window, and I hope Dad has stocked the cooler with Mountain Dew and chocolate bars for s'mores.

Dad and I wave goodbye to Mom and pull out of the driveway.

"So, you talk your mom into drivers ed yet?"

I give Dad a pointed look. "What do you think?"

He chuckles. "I'll try to talk some sense into her. You've got a girlfriend now, right? It's not fair to make her drive everywhere."

"Sure." How do we keep circling back to the one topic I want to avoid? I turn up the radio, killing any chance of conversation, and stare out the window. Out of the corner of my eye I see Dad glancing at me every few seconds.

I close my eyes and relax against the seat. I try to focus on the lyrics to the rock song, and not think about Summer.

Once we arrive at the campsite in the Santa Monica Mountains, we join forces and pitch the tent. Dad's way better at this than I am, but I manage to not rip the canvas or put the stake through my foot, so I call that a win.

We spend the rest of the afternoon exploring the hiking trails. Dad tells me about the latest movie he's been doing stunt work on, and I tell him about school. When we return to our campsite, we start a fire and roast weenies for dinner.

"Dad, how did you know Mom was the one for you?"

He doesn't answer right away, and when I look at him, he's staring pensively into the flames. I can't be sure, but I think maybe he's thinking about happier times with Mom before the divorce. We never really talk about *before*, and I wonder if it makes him sad. It was probably stupid of me to ask.

"I knew your mom was the woman for me the first time I laid eyes on her." He grins. "We were only a little older than you. I saw her walking across the quad on campus and just knew I had to talk to her. After our first date, I knew I wanted to marry her."

Frowning, I think back to what I told Mom after my first date with Summer. *That's the girl I'm going to marry.*

"You going to tell me what happened?" Dad asks, interrupting my thoughts. "Or do I just have to assume the worst."

"Not sure what you mean, Dad." I thrust my stick into the flames and pull it out when the end catches fire.

"Come on, Kane. Your mom told me. What happened with that girl of yours?" I'd hoped he'd let it go, but that clearly isn't happening.

Of course Mom told him. Dad must've been playing dumb, hoping I'd spill on my own. I really don't want to talk about this, but suddenly my mouth has a mind of its own and the whole painful story spews out.

"Hmm."

"Hmm? That's all you've got for me?"

Dad stares into the flames, and I study his face. He narrows his eyes, and the fire casts shadows across him. Coupled with his five o'clock shadow, he looks a little like a cartoon villain. I'd laugh if I wasn't so anxious to hear his advice.

Finally, he turns his face to me. "It sounds like this girl has some baggage you don't know about. Hell, this might not actually have anything to do with you."

"Of course it has to do with me," I grumble, stabbing my stick into the dirt. "I was the one who got dumped, remember?"

"Yes, Kane." I can hear him trying to stay patient with me. "But from what you've said, it sounds to me like she has some other hang up you don't know about."

I throw my arms up. "So how do I win her back?"

Dad grins at me. "Wouldn't it be easier to find some other girl?"

"No." I say firmly, glaring. "She's the only girl I want."

"In that case, I think this calls for a grand gesture."

"Like a flash mob? Come on Dad, you know I can't sing or dance."

He laughs and shakes his head. "That's an example of a grand gesture, but I'll bet you can think of something else. Something she'll really appreciate."

I stare into the flames and think about what Dad's just said. A grand gesture? My mind spins, trying to think of something that will wow Summer and convince her to give us another shot.

30

SUMMER

Slamming the door on Kane was one of the hardest things I've ever done, but I had to do it. I know my words hurt him, but I had to end it before he was in too deep. A little hurt now is better than a lot of hurt later.

And yet, I'm completely miserable without him. His silly texts ended Friday night.

It's been eight days since I broke things off with Kane, and the loneliness has really sunk in. I miss him more than I thought I would, and my resolve is slipping. The only way I could get through foods class this past week was by ignoring him. I couldn't even allow myself to make eye contact. He tried slipping me notes a couple times, but I refused to look for fear of caving.

I think my parents have tuned in to my change in mood, because last night they lifted my grounding a week early.

I've tried sketching, but my inspiration is gone. The last time I opened my sketchbook I was greeted by the sketch of us that I was planning to give him. I ripped the page out and tore it to shreds. Crying, I threw the sketchbook across the room and haven't touched it since.

I've been trying to lose myself in books, but every one I pick up has some element of romance. That just makes me miss Kane more. I'm about ready to give in to bingeing documentaries on Netflix. That should be safe from romance, right?

My phone dings with a text. Closing my eyes, I take a deep breath. Kane is the only one who texts me lately. I shouldn't look. I should block his number. But I'm a masochist, and I look at the screen.

It's not from Kane.

ABIGAIL: Spotting Mark at the beach. I'll be bored to death while he surfs. Keep me company?

I stare at the text. Why would Abigail want me to come after I broke Kane's heart? There's no way she doesn't know about the break up.

I like Abigail. She's not Rachel, but the whole tattoo fiasco aside, she's fun. I hesitate though, wondering if this is a trap to get me to talk to Kane. I'm about to write back with a lie about being busy when another text arrives.

ABIGAIL: Kane is out of town. Pleeeeeeeaaaasssseeee?!?!?!?

Chewing my lip, I wonder if Abigail would lie. But I do recall Kane saying something about spending a weekend with his dad, so I take a chance and write back.

ME: Okay.

I tell Mom where I'm going. She relinquishes her car keys only after I vow not to do anything stupid—like get another tattoo from a sketchy friend of a friend's brother. I slip on my sunglasses and oversized beach hat, then slather myself in my prescription sunscreen before tossing it into my bag and getting in the car.

When I reach the beach, Abigail is sitting in the sand wearing her own floppy sun hat and sunglasses. She gives me a smile when I plop into the sand beside her.

"Thanks for coming," she says.

"Thanks for inviting me." I kick off my flip flops and bury my toes in the sand. I've always loved the feeling of the sun warmed grains sticking to the soles of my feet.

Abigail stares at a tiny spec on the waves, and I realize it's Mark.

"This can get kind of boring when Kane isn't around."

I scoop handfuls of sand and bury my feet to keep busy. I feel like a fraud. An outsider. How can I be friends with her after I hurt Kane? Taking a deep breath, I ask, "Where is Kane?"

"It's his dad's weekend. I'm sure they're doing some activity that has a good chance of injuring him."

So I was right, he's with his dad. I feel a little more relaxed knowing he won't show up today.

We sit in silence for a few minutes, enjoying the sounds of the ocean.

Eventually, Abigail asks if I've had a chance to try a new brand of gel nail polish she saw at Sephora on her last trip into the city. We spend the rest of our time talking about makeup and school.

Ugh. School. When I broke up with Kane, I lost my new friends and lunch table. I couldn't even bring myself to eat at my old table in the shade of the building. The proximity was too close to Kane. I've been eating lunch in the bathroom every day. I can't believe my life has come to this.

An hour or so later, Mark exits the water. He doesn't mention Kane or the breakup, and I'm grateful for that. We say goodbye, and I drive home and lock myself in my bedroom.

Throwing myself across my pink and yellow quilt, I try to hide my tears in my pillow.

For the umpteenth time, I scold myself for ever getting close to Kane in the first place.

31

KANE

By the time Dad drops me off at home, I've come up with the perfect plan to win Summer back. I promise to tell Dad how my grand gesture goes, and I stand at the end of the driveway, waving goodbye until I can no longer see his SUV.

"How was camping?" Mom asks, when I throw open the front door. She glances up from her laptop and looks me over. "I'm happy to see you're still in one piece."

I grin. "It was great. Gotta run, Mom!"

I race down the hall and throw open the door to my bedroom. I barely notice when it bounces off the door stop and slams shut behind me. I throw my camping bag into my dirty laundry hamper and then race out of my room.

In the garage, I rummage through box after box of junk, but I can't find what I'm looking for. After a few minutes, I hear Mom behind me. "What in the world are you doing?"

I swivel and face her. "What happened to that old portable radio?"

She shakes her head, then says, "My old boombox? I got rid of that ages ago. Pretty sure I sold it in one of the neighbors' garage sales. What do you need it for?"

I groan. So much for my grand plan. "Don't worry about it, Mom. It was just an idea I had. I'll think of something else." Before she can say anything, I grab my bike and say, "I'm going to ride around for a bit. I'll be back before dinner."

Peeling out of the driveway, I take off for my old neighborhood. Maybe Mark or Abigail has an old boombox lying around.

I ride like Godzilla is on my tail, and when I reach Mark's driveway I'm panting. I run up to the house and try the doorknob, but it's locked. Mark must not be home.

Cutting across the yard, I nearly trip over a potted plant as I race to Abigail's front door. Before I can try the knob, the door swings open. Abigail is standing there in ripped jeans and an equally ripped tank top.

"Hey," I manage to pant out.

"You okay, Kane?"

I shake my head and push past her into the house. Mark is sitting on the couch, a copy of Surfer Magazine open in his hands. I collapse on the living room area rug, still recovering from my mad dash over. Abigail enters the room a moment later.

"Look, Mark. Kane missed us *so* much he raced over to see us."

"I...need...your help," I pant. My heart rate is finally slowing down, and my breath is coming easier.

"Help with what?" Abigail asks, sitting beside Mark on the couch.

"I need an old boombox so I can get Summer back."

There's a moment of silence, and I look between my friends, who are blinking at me in confusion.

"How is a boombox going to help you get Summer back?" Abigail asks slowly.

"*Say Anything*. It's her favorite. In the movie, Lloyd shows up at Diane's house and holds up the boombox. I'm gonna do that. I'm gonna park my bike outside her house and blast that song from the movie to show her she should give me another chance."

"Just use your phone and a Bluetooth speaker," Abigail says.

I frown. "That's not what he does in the movie. What if she doesn't get the reference."

"Okay, Kane, first of all," Mark says, leaning forward on the couch and staring me in the eye. "*Nobody* has an old boombox like that anymore. That movie is like, thirty years old."

Abigail butts in before Mark can continue. "And second, Summer isn't a moron. If you stand outside her window with *any* speaker playing that song, she's *going* to get the reference." She rolls her eyes, as if to emphasize what an idiot she thinks I am.

I let her words sink in and realize she's probably right. Summer is smart, she'll get it. Now I just have to search the Internet for the name of that song and download it to my phone.

"When do you plan to proclaim your love, Romeo?" Abigail asks.

"As soon as I get the song and some speakers."

Mark shakes his head and picks up his magazine again, but Abigail looks thoughtful. "Come with me. I might have something that will do the trick."

Bike straddled between my legs, I stand by the curb and stare at Summer's house. I feel a moment of hesitation, but it quickly passes. I have to do this. I'm not going to let the girl of my dreams go without a fight.

Abigail told me which window was Summer's, and I position myself beneath it. I'm suddenly grateful for that sleepover they had all those weeks ago.

The Sailor Moon speaker Abigail gave me to use is somewhat embarrassing, but I don't even care. I need to show Summer how much she means to me, even if it means holding up a speaker featuring an anime superhero schoolgirl.

I connect my phone to the speaker, then hold it high while I blast Peter Gabriel's 'In Your Eyes.'

I don't know what I expect to happen. I know what I *hope* will happen.

Summer will come running to the window, grin at me, then run down the stairs and out her front door. She'll throw herself in my arms and we'll kiss and forget she ever dumped me.

I wait for what feels like ages, until I finally see her at the window. She stares at me for a few heartbeats, eyes wide and lips parted, but the smile doesn't come. Retreating from the window, I hope she'll come racing down the stairs, but the door remains firmly shut. When the song ends, I'm left standing outside her bedroom window like an idiot, Sailor Moon speaker in hand and no girl in my arms.

Defeated, I put the speaker back in the bag I carried it in and pedal away. I stop a few houses down and look back, hoping I was premature and she's still coming.

But Summer isn't there.

She isn't coming.

I've lost.

32

SUMMER

Leaning against the wall beside my bedroom window, I squeeze my eyes shut. Is this really happening? Did Kane *really* just recreate the iconic boombox moment from my favorite movie?

Risking another quick glance out the window, I confirm he's definitely out there, a Sailor Moon speaker in hand, playing 'In Your Eyes' at top volume.

I don't know what to do. This is the sweetest thing I've ever seen. Part of me wants to run outside and tell him I was an idiot for letting him go. That the past few weeks with him have been the best I've had in a long time. That I *still* want to be with him.

But an even bigger part of me is screaming that I'm no good for him. And as much as I *want* to run out and throw myself into his arms, I can't. I'm doing this for *him*. So I back away from the wall and lay on my bed, covering my head with my pillow to muffle the music.

I'm grateful my parents are out, and Mandy is at a sleepover. I don't want to have to explain this to anyone. Hopefully my neighbors won't mention anything to my parents. They don't know that

I've broken up with Kane, let alone that I'd been seeing him regularly.

The song ends, and I'm left under a blanket of silence. I wait a little longer before I chance another look out the window. Kane is a few houses down, pedaling away on his bike. He stops and looks back, but I know he can't see me watching, he's too far away. I keep my eyes on him until he rounds the corner, and he's out of sight, then I lay back on my bed and cry.

School last week was hard, and I'm not sure I'm prepared for another week of my self-imposed social isolation. But I suck it up. I don't want to be the sick girl. I've missed too much school already. I will get through this, at least that's what I tell myself.

When I step off the school bus, I scan the crowd of students out front for Kane, Abigail, or Mark. Even though Mark and Abigail were cool to me yesterday, I still want to avoid them.

Abigail's words from our sleepover come back: *Don't hurt him.*

I promised I wouldn't, but that's exactly what I've done.

Like last week, I avoid looking in Mark's direction in chemistry. I swear I can *still* feel the stares and hear the whispers of my peers.

At lunch, I spot Abigail heading toward the lunch line, and I quickly dart out of sight. It's not so much fear of her seeing me, but of her telling Kane. I wait for her to head for the courtyard before entering the line myself.

Feeling brave, I don't hide in the bathroom today. Instead, I find a quiet table in the cafeteria and settle in. I have no appetite. Eventually, I give up on pushing my food around my tray until the bell rings, and I head to class.

Sitting beside Kane every day is stressing me out. I hate that I hurt him. I wish things could be different. But they're not. And it's better for him in the long run. He may hurt a little now, but he'll get over me and move on with someone who isn't a burden. Still, I ignore the notes he tries to pass me and refuse to even look in his direction.

Even though my parents wouldn't approve, I walk home from school. I don't want to wait around for a ride, and I definitely don't want to be surrounded by other kids on the bus.

Cars speed by, students in a hurry to leave school. I turn onto a side street, it's quieter here. Less traffic.

"Pull over!" I hear a girl yell.

I ignore the voice—she's not talking to me—and keep walking. My gaze is fixed on the ground in front of me, ignoring my surroundings.

"What the hell?" This is a male voice, accompanied by tires screeching to a halt. My head whips up, and I realize Abigail and Mark have pulled over a few car lengths ahead of me. Abigail hops out of the passenger side and jogs over.

I nod my head at her, a crappy greeting, but a greeting, nonetheless. Then I ignore her and keep walking, my pace quickening.

"So," she says.

I remain quiet.

She sighs and falls into step beside me, matching my pace. I hear Mark's car creeping along beside us on the street. "Where have you been at lunch?"

I shrug.

"Come on, don't tell me you're hiding in the library to eat. We don't bite."

I shake my head. "They don't allow food in the library." I'm not about to tell her I was eating in the bathroom all last week.

Abigail sighs. "Kane's back, you know."

I keep walking.

"Of course you know. You have class together."

I remain silent.

Abigail heaves a heavy sigh beside me. "Can we have some real talk here? I was hoping you'd say something yesterday, and you didn't, so I'm going to rip off the bandage. Things were good with you and Kane, as far as I can tell. That boy is head over heels in love with you, and you threw him away like yesterday's trash."

Her words fuel the hurt deep inside me, turning it to anger. "You don't know anything!"

"She speaks." Abigail's voice is warm and chipper and calm, as if she'd only said those words to force a reaction from me. Well, it worked. And it helps temper my anger.

I fight back tears and keep walking.

"I know that Kane is heartbroken," she says. "I know that you watched him profess his love to you last night, and you ignored him."

"I had to!" I snap, the words escaping before I can stop them.

"Why?" Abigail's voice is still calm. I was afraid she'd let loose on me like she did on the guy burning the driftwood a few weeks ago, but she doesn't. She's speaking to me like I'm really her friend, not the girl who broke her best friend's heart.

"Because I'm broken. I'm no good for him." My words come out as a whisper the fight having left me with my previous outburst.

"That's bullshit, and I think you know it."

I stare at Abigail, shocked at her words. She rolls her eyes. "We're all a little broken. Why don't you talk to him and let *him* decide if you're no good for him."

"I...I can't." Shaking my head, I walk faster, running away from my problems like always.

Abigail stays beside me, silently keeping me company whether I want her to or not. Mark continues to keep pace beside us in his Subaru.

"Why are you being nice to me?" I finally ask, risking a glance at her.

She blinks, a surprised expression on her face. "Because you're my friend."

I come up short, freezing in place. "I am?"

She rolls her eyes. "Duh. Friends eat lunch and get tattoos together."

I wince, still regretting the tattoo.

She notices, and says, "I never did get a chance to apologize for that. I'm sorry."

I shrug and begin walking again. "Not your fault."

"Next time we get tattoos, we'll go to a reputable place. I know a guy who can get us fake ID's."

I shake my head, unable to stop the corners of my lips from turning up. "I think I'm done with tattoos. I'm lucky my parents didn't kill me."

Abigail grins. "Will you quit running away from your problems and think about talking to Kane? Let *him* decide what he can and can't handle. Please?"

After a pause, I shake my head. "I'll think about it."

The house is almost eerily quiet; I can't even hear my dad snoring down the hall. Everyone has been in bed, sleeping soundly for hours. Except me, of course. My insomnia is in hyperdrive. Even if my disease didn't mess with my ability to sleep at night, I doubt I'd be sleeping anyway.

Abigail's words keep echoing back in my head. Is she right? Should I let Kane decide if I'm worth the trouble? Letting him decide means letting someone outside my family know about my lupus.

But if there's one person I know I can trust, it's Kane. If I tell him and ask him to keep it secret, I know he will. That's not what I'm afraid of.

It's the look of pity my parents and the doctors gave me. I don't think I can bear to see that look on Kane's face.

But, what if he looks at me the same way he always has? What if he doesn't see me differently, and he still wants me? My heart flutters at the idea...but would it be fair to him?

Getting out of bed, I grab my backpack and pull out a notebook. Flipping to a clean page, I begin writing:

Reasons You Shouldn't Want To Be With Me

I scribble my reasons in the notebook. Finally, I put down on paper the number one reason. The confession I've been too afraid to make. Nobody but my parents and sister know what's wrong with me. I have lupus. I will always have lupus. And I will always be a burden on those who love me.

I slam the notebook closed and wipe a tear from the corner of my eye. The thought of letting someone else in terrifies me, but the more I think about it, the more I think maybe Abigail is right. Maybe it should be Kane's choice.

A mixture of calm and uneasiness washes over me as I switch off my bedroom light. The conflicting emotions continue to plague me until sleep finally claims me.

I'm wracked with nerves the following morning. When chemistry ends, I push past my apprehension and approach Mark.

"Hey," I say. "Can I talk to you for a second?"

He looks mildly surprised. I haven't spoken to him since *before*. And even then, I rarely spoke to him without Kane present. I like Mark, but like me, he's quiet.

"Sure," he says. He grabs his books from the lab table and gives me his full attention.

"I need a favor..." I bite my lower lip. What if Mark hates me for breaking up with Kane? He didn't say anything at the beach, but we're alone now. No Abigail around to witness.

"Okay..." he prompts.

I backtrack. "Do you know what Abigail said to me?"

He pauses and looks uncomfortable. "...Yes."

I chew my lip again, then release it. "I'm going to take her advice."

Mark's eyebrows shoot up in surprise. "Oh." He smiles, his face relaxing. "Good." Then he frowns. "But what's the favor?"

"Can you get Kane to the skatepark after school?"

Mark casts his gaze heavenward. When he looks at me again, he looks wary. "He hasn't gone out with us since..." He lets the sentence trail. We both know what he means. "But I'll try."

It's the best I can hope for.

33

KANE

S itting at my lunch table in the courtyard, I swirl a french fry through the mound of ketchup on my tray. I know I'm moping. I'm trying really hard to be my usual upbeat self, but I'm failing miserably.

I had the girl of my dreams, and I lost her. I was so sure that playing the song outside her bedroom window would change her mind. That she would realize what she means to me. There wasn't a second that I doubted it.

Until she turned her back on me, leaving me standing alone like an idiot in the street with that Sailor Moon speaker.

I try to ignore the looks my friends are giving each other when they think I'm not looking.

"Skatepark, Kane?" Abigail's voice breaks through my pity party.

"Huh?" I feel like there's more to the question than what I heard.

"After school, are you coming with us to the skatepark?"

I shrug. Every day they've been asking me to come with them. To the skatepark, the beach, to hang at their houses. Every time I tell them no.

"You're coming."

My head jerks up, and my mouth hangs open, surprised at the force behind Mark's words.

Abigail gives him a stern look. He rolls his eyes at her before turning back to me.

"You need to snap out of this," he says. "Giving up everything you love is only going to make you feel worse. Come with us. Get back on your board and try to nail that rail grind again."

I stare at my fries; lunch is nearly over and they're as cold as they are soggy. Sighing, I nod. "Okay."

"Okay?" Abigail's voice is hopeful.

I let out a deep gust of breath and say, more angrily than I intend, "Yeah, I said okay, all right? I'll be there."

Mark smirks. "Good."

Stepping through the arch of the skatepark, it's like I'm taking my first full breath in weeks. The scent of the fries wafting toward me from the food stand is as familiar as antiseptic and bandages. As soon as I'm standing on my board, flying across the concrete, I realize how much I've missed it. I may not have Summer, but Mark is right, giving up other things I love isn't going to make me feel any better.

I glance around and see Abigail and Mark near the benches. Abigail is giving me a thumbs up, and Mark is watching me intently. My gaze travels around the park, and I nearly fall off my board. I must be hallucinating. I swear I just saw Summer standing near the entrance, watching me.

Shaking my head, I focus on what's in front of me. Now is no time for my mind to be playing tricks on me. I inhale deeply...exhale...force my concentration on the obstacles around me. I put myself in the zone. There's only me, my board, and the smooth concrete beneath my wheels.

I kick against the ground, gathering the speed I crave. The rail is in sight, and when the time is right, I kick the board into the air. The board's truck connects with the metal. There's nothing but me, my board, and this rail. I will not fail this time.

It's over in a matter of seconds. I slide out of the grind. My feet are still on the board when it slams onto the pavement, and suddenly the world comes back. Mark and Abigail are clapping and cheering for me, and I grin. I haven't felt this happy since before Summer dumped me. I bring my board to a stop a few feet away from my friends.

"Holy shit, man." Mark shakes his head, grinning. "You actually nailed it."

Abigail is staring off toward the entrance, her expression cautiously optimistic. I follow her gaze, and my sight lands on Summer. She isn't a hallucination after all. My exuberance at landing the rail grind is forgotten, one thought has taken over my mind: *What is she doing here?*

"Hey, Abz," Mark says. "Let's go grab some carne asada fries."

I glance at him, and he's beaming like the cat that ate the canary. He grabs Abigail by the arm and drags her toward the food stand.

Hesitantly, I turn toward Summer. While my attention was diverted, she entered the park, stopping only a few feet away from me. She's wearing her taco shirt, the one I had made for her. What does *that* mean?

"Hi, Kane," she says softly, staring at a piece of paper clutched tightly in both hands.

"Hey," I reply. I want to throw my arms around her and kiss her, but she's not my girlfriend anymore.

Summer fidgets with the paper, and I shove one hand in my pocket.

"I'm sorry," she says. "I know I hurt you, but I did it *for* you. I'm no good for you, Kane."

"That's not true, Summer." My eyes, stinging at the painful reminder, plead with her, but she has yet to actually look at me.

"*Yes*, it is," she insists, meeting my eyes for the first time. She bites her lower lip and fidgets with the paper again.

"What's that?" I ask, gesturing to the paper.

She takes a deep breath then exhales. Staring at the paper, she says, "I know how much you like your top five lists. So here's one for you." She pauses to inhale deeply once more. "My top five reasons for why I'm terrible for you, and you would be better off finding someone else."

I did *not* see this coming. I take a moment to absorb her words, then say, "I bet they're all terrible reasons. Try me."

I see the corner of her mouth twitch upward, it's a tiny movement before her expression returns to neutral. She begins.

"Number Five: I'm prone to moodiness."

I scoff. "And I'm prone to injury. We've all got our flaws."

She licks her lips and continues. "Four: I'm not nearly as funny or brave as you are."

"Of course not. I'm the funny, you're the brains and beauty. It's all about balance."

She meets my gaze. "Three: I don't have the best track record when it comes to relationships. I tend to screw things up and I'm told I have a habit of running away from my problems."

I roll my eyes. "Breaking up with me is the only thing you've done to screw this up, but we can easily fix that."

Her forehead scrunches, as if in thought, and she pulls her lower lip between her teeth again. I want her to stop that. I don't want her to be nervous talking to me.

"Two: I don't skateboard or do bike tricks or any of that stuff you're into."

I wave her off. "So what? I can teach you." Her reaction is

SOMETHING I'M GOOD AT

comically skeptical. "Or you can cheer from the stands and drive me to urgent care."

She cracks a smile, but it falters as she looks back at her list. Her breath is shaky, and the silence hovers between us. Then she closes her eyes, seeming to brace herself, and crumples the list in her fist. I count each second, waiting.

One. Two. Three...

"What's number one?" I finally ask.

"The number one reason you shouldn't want to be with me..." Her eyes are still closed, and she takes another shaky breath. Finally, her eyes open and meet mine. "I have lupus, Kane. There is no cure, and I will be sick for the rest of my life."

My mouth opens, then closes. She's surprised me again. I've heard of lupus. Sometimes we get postcards in the mail asking for donations to the Lupus Foundation, but I don't know anything about it.

Summer holds my gaze, and I try to form my thoughts into words. Finally, I speak. "Summer, I'm not going to lie and tell you I know *anything* about lupus. But I do know this, I don't care if you have scales and a tail. I'm sure you've realized by now that I'm a little crazy at times, but you make me sane. So, tell me all about lupus, and let me be there for you."

Summer shakes her head slowly back and forth, tears in her eyes. "You don't know what you're asking."

I take a small step forward and smile. "I'm asking to be with the girl I love."

She sniffles, wiping her eyes with the back of her hand. "You love me?"

I hate seeing her cry, so I close the distance between us, stopping so we're toe to toe. "Duh."

She laughs, but because she's crying it comes out as a snort. She presses her forehead to my chest, and I wrap my arms around her.

"Kane, you have to understand." Between the tears and her

face against my chest, her voice is muffled. "This isn't something I'll ever get over. I'll have it for the rest of my life. I'm giving you an out, before you have to deal with any of that."

I wait for her to say more. She doesn't.

"Are you done trying to tell me how I should think and feel?"

She doesn't say anything, but I feel her nod.

"Good. Can I kiss you now?" I lift her chin with my hand, forcing her eyes to meet mine.

"I'm covered in tears and snot," she protests, sniffling.

"I'm usually covered in blood and dirt. Do you really think I care about tears and snot?"

She laughs again, and I press my lips to hers. I can taste her teardrops, and I wasn't lying when I said I don't care. I'm just glad she's here in my arms again.

EPILOGUE

One Month Later

I hardly recognize the girl staring back at me in the full-length mirror. The blue dress I never got to wear to Homecoming looks even better than I remember. But that could have something to do with my new outlook on life.

Abigail steps into view, grinning from behind me at my reflection. "Kane's jaw is going to drop."

"Thanks." I admire her dress, the black one with the red detailing that she also never wore to Homecoming. "You look great too."

She beams, then checks the time on her phone. "The guys should be here any minute. I still can't believe you and Kane are making me go to a school dance."

"Shut up. You know you're excited."

"Summer!" Mandy's bellowing can probably be heard at the end of the block. "Your *boyfriend's here!*"

Abigail and I exchange a look, then laugh at my sister's teasing sing-song voice.

"Go ahead," I tell her. "I'll catch up in a minute, okay?"

Abigail nods, then grabs her clutch from my bed and leaves.

When the room is clear, I give my hair and makeup one final inspection in the mirror. Today feels like a second chance for me. I'd ruined Homecoming for my friends, especially Kane, but tonight we'll have a second chance with the Winter Ball.

There's a soft knock at my door, and I spin around. Mom is standing in my doorway, beaming at me.

"You look beautiful, honey." She presses her hands to her chest, as if she's so moved by the sight of me she has to physically hold in her emotions.

"Thanks, Mom."

"I'm really proud of you," she tells me.

I blink in surprise. *She is? Why?*

My bafflement must be obvious, because she goes on. "You've had a rough time since your diagnosis. You were doing a pretty good job faking it when school started, you almost had me fooled. But this past month, I can see that things have truly changed. You're not pretending anymore, you really are happy again."

I smile, feeling a blush creep into my cheeks. My hair is up, so I have nowhere to hide. "I am happier," I mumble. And that's the truth. Having my secret out in the open has taken a weight off my shoulders. Kane has been an amazing support, even going so far as to research lupus on his own, then come to me with questions. Eventually, I confided in Abigail and Mark too. Abigail hugged me and apologized again for the whole tattoo incident.

Mom steps into my room and pulls me into her arms, careful not to mess my hair and makeup. When she releases me, she's smiling. "You'd better get downstairs. That boy is quite antsy to see you."

I can't stop my grin, and I know I'm blushing deeper than before.

Mom gives me one last smile, then leaves. I grab my clutch, phone, and shawl, then follow her. At the top of the staircase, I can hear Kane and Abigail bickering, as usual. I smile to myself and begin my descent down the stairs.

Halfway down, the noise stops, and I feel five pairs of eyes on me. When I reach the landing, Kane is standing a mere three feet away, while the others hang back.

He's frozen in place for a moment, his mouth hanging open, as Abigail predicted. "You look amazing," he finally says, sending the all too familiar blush creeping into my cheeks once more.

"Thanks. You clean up pretty nicely yourself."

Kane grins and adjusts his pale blue bow tie. He looks amazing in his charcoal suit with white dress shirt. "I got you this," he says, holding out a clear box with a corsage. "I got you the wrist kind. I figured there was less chance of stabbing you this way." He opens the top and steps forward to slip it around my wrist.

I laugh, then feel a tap on my other arm. I glance over and see Mandy holding the box with the boutineer I bought for Kane.

"This one has a pin," Mandy says, addressing Kane. "So I guess you'd better have someone else put it on you."

We all laugh, and Mandy beams. I take the boutineer out of the box and step closer to pin it to Kane's lapel.

"Thanks." He takes my hand in his and squeezes it gently.

"Picture time," Mom announces cheerfully, ushering us all outside. Once we're positioned in front of the garden, Kane puts his arm around my shoulders. We smile as Mom takes an obscene number of photos in every possible group combination she can think of, as well as individual shots. Even Mandy insisted on getting in some of the photos.

"Mom, we have to get going," I complain, as she snaps a photo of Kane and Mark, posing like tough guys with their arms crossed and sunglasses on.

"Okay, okay," Mom relents, putting away her camera.

"I want copies of those," Kane says to Mom, as he walks past her to stand by my side. Her eyes light up, and I know without a doubt that she approves of my boyfriend. I feel a little guilty having kept him a secret for so long.

Kane and I slide into the backseat of Mark's car. "You've got your meds?" he whispers, his breath tickling my neck. Even though Mark and Abigail know about my disease, it's sweet that Kane continues to try and respect my privacy.

I nod and give him a peck on the cheek. "I'm good, thanks."

He takes my hand and squeezes it. Kane has really surprised me, in a good way, since I told him about my lupus. He's constantly looking out for me now, and always reminding me that it's okay to say no in order to conserve my energy for the stuff that really matters. I'm constantly wondering why I ever worried about telling him in the first place.

The banquet hall is a beautiful winter wonderland. Fairy lights and shimmery white tulle are strung from the ceiling, and crystal snowflakes dangle and sparkle like ice. You'd never know that just outside the doors is the Southern California coastline.

During dinner, our group of four sits at a table with two other couples from school, nobody we know well though. We mostly ignore the other group, and they do the same. After dinner, the staff clears the tables away and the dance begins.

Kane and I drag Mark and Abigail onto the dance floor and force them to dance with us. They're both clearly out of their element, but they seem to be having fun. When a slow song begins,

Mark holds out a hand to Abigail and she accepts. I watch them for a moment, as they turn in slow circles, laughing.

I turn to Kane, standing beside me, and realize he's watching me. "Do I have food on my face?"

"I just like to look at you," he says, his face holding one of his rare serious expressions.

I shake my head and laugh. He's used this line on me before. "Dance with me?"

"Always." He places his hands at my waist. I drape my arms over his shoulders, clasping my hands behind his neck, my body flush against his.

"Finally," he mumbles against my ear. "I've been waiting to slow dance with you for way too long."

"All you had to do was ask."

"Now you tell me!"

Laughing, I rest my cheek against his shoulder and enjoy this peaceful moment. I will always be a girl with lupus, but tonight, I am just a regular girl dancing with her boyfriend.

The song ends, and we only break apart when the people around us bump into us. Laughing, I take Kane's hand and lead him off the dance floor.

"Are you having fun?" he asks.

"I am."

"Good. Me too."

I look around, trying to memorize every detail.

"I'll be back in a few, okay?" I tell him.

Kane nods, and I head off toward the restroom. Once inside, I approach the mirror and check my makeup. I may have told my friends about my lupus, but I still don't want my butterfly rash on display for everyone to see.

I touch up my makeup, and as I'm closing my clutch, the door swings open. In the mirror, my eyes lock with Rachel's.

She's wearing a brilliant red dress, and it contrasts beautifully with her black hair and tan skin. Her mouth opens in surprise. Apparently, she didn't expect to see me in here.

Before she can speak, I say, "You look really pretty tonight, Rachel."

It's time for me to let go of the past. I need to quit holding this grudge and move on.

"Thanks," she says, after a moment of hesitation. "You do too."

"Can we talk for a minute?" I ask, chewing my lower lip.

"Yeah." Her reply is hesitant, as if she's afraid of what I might say.

"I've been thinking a lot lately," I begin. "And I forgive you."

Rachel sucks in a sharp breath. "Really?" Her expression is a cross between relief and trepidation.

I shake my head. "I don't know if I can ever fully trust you again, but I want to move on and make peace."

"I hope someday I can earn your trust back. The kiss was two seconds, and I ended it as soon as I realized what was happening. I never meant for it to happen, or to hurt you. I really *am* sorry, Summer."

I shake my head and force a smile. "It's in the past now. Let's just..." I trail off, searching for the right words. "Let's try being casual friends and go from there."

"Casual friends," Rachel repeats. "I guess that's better than whatever we've been these last six months."

"Casual friends then." I glance at the door behind me. "I'd better get back to my date."

She nods, and I turn to leave.

"Hey, Summer?"

I turn my head back to face her.

"I'm really happy for you," she says. "Kane is crazy about you, and you seem really good together."

"Thanks." I exit the bathroom and find Kane sitting right where I left him.

"All good?" he asks, standing up and wrapping me in a hug.

"Yes," I say, and with a start, I realize that I feel lighter. Maybe I should've forgiven Rachel sooner. But no, I wasn't ready then. It took Kane accepting me, broken as I am, for me to learn to accept myself and let go of the past. "Let's go dance."

Join Caroline's newsletter and stay up to date with her writing.

(*She promises not to flood your inbox.*)

www.carolineandrus.com

—

Read Rachel's version of what happened at prom in **Kick Ass Girls of Fire & Ice: Proms & Balls**, available for **free** wherever ebooks are sold!

—

Don't miss your next favorite book!

Join the Fire & Ice mailing list

www.fireandiceya.com/mail.html

THANK YOU FOR READING

Did you enjoy this book?

We invite you to leave a review at the website of your choice, such as Goodreads, Amazon, Barnes & Noble, etc.

DID YOU KNOW THAT LEAVING A REVIEW...

- Helps other readers find books they may enjoy.
- Gives you a chance to let your voice be heard.
- Gives authors recognition for their hard work.
- Doesn't have to be long. A sentence or two about why you liked the book will do.

PLAYLIST

Something I'm Good At - Brett Eldredge
Young & Crazy - Frankie Ballard
What Ifs - Kane Brown & Lauren Alaina
Please Don't Fall For Me - Marit Larsen
Crazier - Taylor Swift
Rain Falls - Skrizzly Adams
Love Goes Boom - Bowling For Soup
Chicks Dig It - Chris Cagle
More - Hunter Hayes
This Ain't My Day - Bowling For Soup
Arms - Christina Perri
Die a Happy Man - Thomas Rhett
Best Shot - Jimmie Allen
Speechless - The Veronicas
Balance Beam - Blue October
Delusional - Charlie Allen
I Don't Want To Talk About It - Marit Larsen
I Would - Lower Than Atlantis
The Light - Disturbed
Nobody But Me - Michael Bublé
Niki FM - Hawthorn Heights

Listen to the playlist on Spotify!
http://bit.ly/SIGApl

AUTHOR'S NOTE

When I was first playing with the idea of writing this story, I spoke with my friend, Alisha Webster, to get some general information about what life is like living with lupus.

Sure, I'd seen what my sister, who also has lupus, has gone through, but I wanted another source of first person information on the disease.

One of the first things Alisha told me about was The Spoon Theory, which Summer mentions early on in the story.

To read the full theory, written by Christine Miserandino, please visit:

www.butyoudontlooksick.com/articles/written-by-christine/the-spoon-theory

—

To learn more about lupus, or to donate to help educate others and search for a cure, please visit the the Lupus Foundation of America.

www.lupus.org

ACKNOWLEDGMENTS

It took over a year to write this book, and I could never have done it without the constant nagging—I mean encouragement—from my writing partner in crime, Rachel Walter. Thank you Rachel. I don't know what I'd do without you. (Probably never finish anything!)

A big thank you to my friend Alisha Webster and my sister Katie Schumacher for answering my questions about Lupus. I hope this story helps shed some light on some of your struggles.

A huge shout out to my beta readers: Alisha Webster, Maggie Douglas, Xavier Douglas, Jenn Garey, and Heidi Ketchum - thank you for being among the first eyes on my story and offering your feedback to help make this book stronger.

Thank you to my family for not being *too* annoyed when I locked myself in my office for hours on end because "MOM NEEDS TO WORK!"

Thank you to my mom, Nancy Schumacher, for the constant support and for editing all of my books.

Thank you Jess Brytowski for helping name my fictional town of Sol del Mar, California.

And to you, reader, your support means the world. Thank you.

ABOUT THE AUTHOR

Caroline Andrus was born and raised in the St. Paul suburbs where she still lives with her husband, two daughters, and Henry McCoy—a wild cougar trapped in the body of a house cat.

When she's not reading or writing, you can find her working out, playing dumb phone games, or catching up on Netflix.

Since 2011 she has been second in command for indie press Melange Books. She is head of acquisitions for their YA imprint, Fire & Ice Young Adult books, as well as web designer, formatter, and head of their cover art department.

She is passionate about both reading and writing teen fiction, and is pretty sure she will forever be eighteen at heart.

Join Caroline's newsletter and stay up to date with her writing.

(*She promises not to flood your inbox.*)

www.carolineandrus.com

Caroline would love to hear from you!
Connect with her online:

www.carolineandrus.com
www.carolineandrus.com/blog

facebook.com/caroline_andrus

twitter.com/AndrusCaroline

instagram.com/caroline_andrus

amazon.com/author/carolineandrus

goodreads.com/carolineandrus

bookbub.com/authors/caroline-andrus